Tales of the Happy Frog

The Beginnings

by William Martin

Also by William Martin

(Traditionally published non fiction)

The Parent's Tao Te Ching

The Couple's Tao Te Ching

The Sage's Tao Te Ching

A Path and a Practice

The Tao of Forgiveness

The Caregiver's Tao Te Ching (with Nancy Martin)

The Activist's Tao Te Ching (May, 2016)

(Ebook editions)

30 Days of Tao

Lost in the Tao

Day by Day With the Tao Te Ching

The Wheel Will Turn

Walking the Tao

The Time is Tao

Paperback edition by NW Bookbinding

www.nwbookbinding.com

www.taoistliving.com
PO Box 982
Mount Shasta, California 96067

Introduction

The challenge of weaving a world from the threads of my own imagination has been the greatest writing adventure of my life. Expressing ideas, ideals, hopes, and dreams in a fictional form turns out to be the most vulnerable of all writing experiences. It has been a wonderful journey into my thoughts and dreams, a journey I hope to take often in the future.

I have discovered a deep appreciation for all fiction writers who have inspired me over the years. I also have a profound awe for their ability to inspire, encourage, and engross the reader through the creation of stories. I hope that my own venture into these waters will provide a small echo of their wonderful gifts and that the world of *The Happy Frog* will bring some small glimpses of hope and encouragement to all who share my longing for a "New Paradigm" - a new and humane way of living on this Earth. May the fictional world of Cooper, Connie, Mary, Carl and all the others in Carson Beach be an archetype for the real world we may one day make together.

Bill Martin
Mount Shasta, CA 2017

For my daughter, Lara.

A wonderful writer and gifted storyteller.

Chapter 1 - Ker-Plunk

The old pond
a frog jumps in
ker-plunk!
Basho

Carl stood in the chill of the summer fog that had yet to give way to the late morning sun. A week of driving west had brought him as far in that direction as he could go. Leaning against his white Mazda pickup and squinting his eyes as he peered between the buildings, he could just make out the surf rolling in along Carson Beach. *So that's the Pacific Ocean,* he thought, *Peaceful Ocean. Must have seemed that to sailors rounding the Horn.* He chuckled to himself, thinking that he might have just sailed round a Horn of his own, but one beyond which there may be dragons.

"What in the hell am I doing here?" he wondered aloud.

No answer came from amidst the sound of surf and gulls. Even though he had driven only a few hundred miles each day, stopping early for motel, fast food, TV, beer, and sleep, he had managed to cover two thousand miles without really putting his thoughts into any coherent order. Each day's drive was all he thought about. Attending to traffic and somewhat to the unfolding countryside had supplied enough stimulus to keep the nattering voices of his mind at bay during the trip. As long as he was heading somewhere for the day, he was able to reach an agreement with his mind that nothing else would be considered. Now, at the edge of the Pacific Ocean, would the cacophony of voices return? Of course it would.

It started a week ago on a Saturday morning. He awoke around 6:30 with the dream still in his mind. It was a dream that had been repeating night after night; a pair of bare feet dancing on the beach, dancing to a wild unrecognizable tune. Above the feet he could see the folds of some sort of dress or robe swaying and rippling in the breeze of the dance. The feet of a man or a woman? He couldn't tell. He wanted to join in the dance, but he couldn't feel his own feet. He couldn't get a sense of the sand beneath him. He began to panic and wonder if he even had legs... then an abrupt waking into the summer sun breaking through the folds of his bedroom curtain.

He sighed as he swung his legs over the side of the bed and was strangely comforted to feel his bare feet touch the carpet. He flexed his toes against the pile of the old shag throw rug. *Dancing on the beach.* No one danced on beaches in Grand Rapids. There were no nearby beaches, but if there had been, no one would dance on them. If there had been beaches one would, at most, stroll sedately along them. Dancing would not be in the picture at all. One might stroll in prayerful communion with Jesus but not often, lest one's religion turn toward emotionalism or worse, mysticism.

An hour later Carl was at his fiancee's house, sitting at the kitchen table sipping Folger's instant coffee and listening to Amy go over the invitation list for their coming September wedding. Amy was a computer analyst with Amway Corporation, one of the largest employers in Grand Rapids. She insisted that she did not buy into the Amway marketing scheme, which was a prettied-up version of the old pyramid scam. She was merely a computer expert making a good salary from a large corporation. Carl told himself he was fine with that, but on the occasions he had accompanied Amy to company events he felt as if he had fallen into a dream-like episode of Twilight Zone in which the hero was surrounded by almost-human doppelgängers who spoke English words that individually had meaning but that were arranged in sentences that made no sense whatsoever.

Carl taught two elective classes in Art at Grand Rapids Christian High School and coached the school's cross country and track and field teams. This paid him about a half of a living wage. He earned another quarter from the free-lance painting classes he would lead at churches and community centers around the city and from the occasional painting that he would sell for a few dollars. The remaining quarter was a puzzle that never seemed to yield a solid solution. It left him with the feeling that there must be some pieces missing, perhaps just one piece.

The accusation that Amy's salary was that missing piece would occasionally float to the surface of his mind and be quickly dismissed. Amy was perfect for him. They had been friends through college, though they never dated then. Carl and Maggie were the ideal couple during their days at Michigan State and Amy was one of Maggie's best friends. With graduation, when relationships end in marriage or in tears, Carl and Maggie's ended in tears, at least on Carl's part. Amy had been there to console him. Amy's degree in computer science led to her choice of job opportunities. She took a position with Amway, moved to Grand Rapids, and began to share a large house with several co-workers. Carl's degree in fine arts led to one tentative, part-time, temporary job offer from Grand Rapids Christian High School and the suggestion from his parents that he move back to his old room - just until he got on his feet. He took the job offer and managed to avoid the housing suggestion.

Carl and Amy made love for the first time on Christmas Eve. He had been surprised and delighted at her sexual hunger for him. All the issues that might have arisen from his break-up with Maggie and his uncertainty about his future in art or anything else quieted down and retreated to the darker places of his consciousness. No need to be unhappy. No need to struggle. No need to ponder. No need to even sleep alone. That they would eventually marry was tacitly understood during the four and a half years that had elapsed. Now, what had been tacit had become formally acknowledged and Amy was in full-blown planning and organizing mode.

"You're not listening."

Carl pulled his mind back from the moonlit beach of his dream and blinked. "Sorry, I drifted off for a minute."

"You do that a lot lately. Are you having second thoughts?"

"About what?"

"About us," she said coldly.

"No," he said quickly. "No, not at all, honey." He reached for her hand but did not reach quickly enough as she moved it to her lap, crumpling the invitation list in her fist.

Her lip quavered as she sat continuing to wad the list into a small ball. "You don't want to get married. I just know it."

"Of course I do."

As he formed these four words in his mind, he sincerely meant them. By the time they had escaped his lips, he realized that he did not mean them. His breath caught in his chest and he leaned back in his chair. The image of feet dancing in the moonlight suddenly filled his mind. Wild music echoed in his ears. His heart began to pound in a disturbingly rapid rhythm.

"You do?" she looked at him, still wadding the list in her hands.

Silence. Music, Dancing feet. Pounding heart. Not breathing.

Oh my God!, they both thought simultaneously.

As he walked down the steps of the large faux-Victorian house where Amy and her roommates lived, Carl could hear the sound of her weeping coming through the open kitchen window. A voice screamed in the back of his head, *"Stop, you idiot! She loves you. The sex is great. You won't have to worry about money ever again."* Then the voice unleashed a salvo that almost stopped him in his tracks. *"You won't make it without her."*

But he managed to continue down the sidewalk to his ten-year old Mazda pickup with a camper shell covering the bed. He unlocked the door, climbed in, fastened his seat belt and drove one block to the Chevron station by the freeway entrance. He filled the tank, using his emergency credit card, washed the windshield, and bought a bottle of Starbuck's iced Mocha. He returned to the truck, turned on the ignition, and sat for a moment before pulling out of the station.

His mind remained in a state of shock that was quiet and almost restful as he pulled up to the duplex that had been his home for the past four years. He carefully kept from thinking about anything as he quickly packed two suitcases, a duffel bag, and a gym bag with the majority of his clothing. He also packed his briefcase with his MacBook laptop computer, checkbook, passport, and the cache of $825 he had put away in the bottom left corner of his sock drawer. He then carefully packed his sketch pads, colored pencils, brushes, easel, palates, water colors, and oils in a wicker basket.

Part of his brain was screaming like the anguished soul on the road in Edvard Munch's powerful painting. Another part was calm and focused on the few things he knew he wanted to do. He shut off the gas at the meter outside and wrote a note to Carlos Montoya, the landlord who lived with his wife and three year old son in the adjoining duplex, saying that he was leaving on sudden business and would call in a few days.

He taped the note on the Montoya's door, locked the door to his duplex, loaded his bags and paint supplies in his truck, started the engine and was reassured by the truck's reliable response. He looked back at the little duplex with the Montoya children's toys scattered around the lawn. He scanned his feelings for a sign that he was being foolish, a voice that would offer a reasonable alternative, a more responsible action. Finding no such voice, he drove down Elm Street to DeVos Avenue, turned right three blocks to the freeway, and took the Westbound on-ramp heading toward the Pacific Ocean two thousand miles away.

"What the hell am I doing here?" Carl asked aloud again of the fog shrouded street. And again no answer came from the surf and sand. "No money. Bridges burning all the way from here to Michigan. What the hell am I doing?"

Across the street he noticed a small wooden sign hanging on a post by a garden gate. It was carefully carved with two Chinese characters on the right side, outlined in red. On the left were carved the words, "Happy Frog Cafe - Welcome Weary Traveler."

Carl's eyebrows raised, *Welcome weary traveler?* He stood for a moment contemplating the connection between the sign and his own situation. He thought it must be a reference to the tourist business a beach town needs. Then he shrugged his shoulders, *Well, I'm hungry, a traveler, and certainly a weary one.*

He crossed the street and stood for a moment by the small wooden sign and the path that led to a green and white three-story building set back about 100 feet. Large flat stones were laid in what appeared to be a random pattern to form the path. The plants along the path looked as if they arrived there of their own free will, having seeded the wind and blown along the coast until they found just this spot to make a home. They seemed to say, "we've never seen the inside of a nursery." Yet, as he walked up the path, Carl felt that they might be situated according to a careful plan, a plan designed to create an environment that would subtly relax the person entering the path; that would suggest a sense of space and freedom while still guiding one along in a certain direction.

To the right of the front door, in a large shallow ceramic bowl containing Irish moss and small waterfall fountain, sat a statue of a frog. About a foot high, the frog sat in the lotus position, froggy hands resting comfortably on a fat little belly. On his face was a mysterious, naughty, and appealing smile, somehow communicated by the sculptor with a few simple curved lines. Carl smiled in response. He felt a strange sensation, as if he were about to enter a place where he was somehow known and where people were waiting for him, almost like the Boston bar, *Cheers*, of vintage TV fame, "where they're always glad you came." For a moment he had the disquieting sensation that the little stone creature had been waiting for him here at the westernmost terminus of his journey, that it knew a secret of some sort. He opened the door to the cafe.

Chapter 2 - Call Me Coop

James F. Cooper ("Call me Coop," he would say, "The F is none of anyone's business, but be assured it is not Fenimore.") was head cook and owner of The Happy Frog Cafe. He had purchased it four years ago from Mary O'Hara and Connie Delaney, who began serving meals fifteen years earlier in the living room of what had been Mary's family home. Connie and Mary still lived on the upper floors of the old building and Connie worked most days as Cooper's waitress, assistant cook, and resident fey woman. Mary, educated as a veterinarian at the University of Oregon, spent four days each week, plus on-call days, as Director of Animal Medicine at the Oregon Wildlife Refuge, twenty miles south of Carson Beach. Together, Cooper, Connie, and Mary formed a trinity of benevolent oddness in an already somewhat odd oceanside town.

On this particular morning Cooper was standing by the grill counter chopping tomatoes, garlic, and onions for pasta sauce and Connie was cleaning up after a surge of late breakfast business. She looked up from wiping down a table as the door opened, causing a small delicate chime to sound. A tall young man with dark hair and a green raincoat stood in the doorway for a moment as if wondering what to do next. Connie walked quickly over to the door and greeted him.

"Hello. Come on in. You look tired and hungry... The clam chowder should be ready. That, along with some garlic bread and a nice pot of Jasmine Pearl tea would be just the thing. Come on over here by the window and sit down. I'll get the tea right away. The bathroom is over there to the back behind that screen. Let me hang up your coat."

Carl stood immobile for a moment as the slim blond woman took his coat and her torrent of words poured over him. "Uh..." he managed to articulate before being led by the arm to a small wooden table by a window that looked north down the beach. He sat for a moment and then realized that he indeed needed the bathroom.

As he made his way through the arrangement of tables, plants, and shoji screens he was only vaguely aware of other patrons scattered at various tables in the large windowed room. He found the bathroom to be a cozy paneled room complete with a wooden water tank perched high above the toilet just like Thomas Crapper's original invention.

He returned to the table to find a blue-green pottery mug sitting beside a matching tea pot along with a bowl of raw sugar and a pitcher of cream. The hostess, or whoever she was, was just setting out utensils. She appeared older than Carl had initially assumed but her svelte figure and ease of movement gave her a air of youth. Maybe not youth, really, but some aura of grace and lightness that seemed almost fairy-like. Attractive, but somewhat unsettling.

"My name's Connie," she said as he sat back down. He noticed she omitted the standard, "I'll be your server."

"Hello, Connie," he responded automatically, "I'm Carl de Wilde"

"Where are you from, Carl?" she asked.

"Grand Rapids, Michigan," Carl said. *Grand Rapids. God. What am I doing here? What...?*

"Well," she raised her eyebrows a bit, "You're a long way from home... " She paused, "... or are you? ..." She continued, "Well, Carson Beach is a good place to look for things."

Carl frowned. "I don't..."

Connie patted his shoulder again, "See now, I'm making you uncomfortable. I'll just go get your clam chowder."

"I really didn't order..."

"I think you'll enjoy it. I'll be right back." She moved quickly, but without hurrying, back to the grill area and ladled a large bowl full of chowder. The man behind the grill counter smiled in Carl's direction as he set out an order of garlic bread which she took along with the chowder back to the bemused Carl.

"Try it. You'll like it." she smiled and went back to her clean-up work.

Carl sighed and tasted a spoonful of chowder. It was rich, creamy, and full of tender clams. He glanced around at the room. Tables similar to the wooden table at which he sat were scattered through what at first glance appeared to be one large room, but he noticed evidence in the structure that it had been perhaps three rooms at one time. Each table was situated with a degree of privacy through the use of potted plants, screens, and the nooks formed by partial walls and cabinets. It was spacious and cozy at the same time.

Carl noticed that the man standing behind the grill counter chopping something was wearing an Oregon State cap, a University of Oregon sweatshirt, and an apron proclaiming the virtues of Williams University, wherever and whatever that was. The man looked up as Carl was staring at his divided loyalties. He caught Carl's eye and winked, touching his cap with his knife.

Where am I? Carl wondered.

"He's lost, you know," Connie whispered to Cooper as she loaded dishes into the Hobart dishwasher.

Cooper kept his attention on the onions he was dicing. "Who's lost?"

"The young man over by the window."

"Lost as in needing a GPS, or lost in the mazes of his mind?"

"There's just something about him that feels lost to me, that's all," she exclaimed, then tossed her head and flounced back into the cafe.

Which means she wants me to take some action, thought Cooper, *to get involved somehow; to be helpful.* He was reluctant to venture into the morass of taking action, especially "helpful" action. It often backfired. It was unwise. It was contrary to his intellectual principles. And he usually did it anyway.

He looked up and saw the young man paying for his lunch and listening to more clucking advice from mother hen Connie. As he watched him wander out the door and pause to look at the Happy Frog statue, Cooper realized, *Yeah, lost all right. I know the feeling kid.*

Connie drifted back to the grill and stood by Cooper. "I sent him over to look at the cabin on Filbert Street. Maybe he'd like to rent it. I think he'd like to stay in town awhile." she said, not looking at Cooper.

Cooper sighed, "Connie, I know you have a sense of these things, but leave me out of your psychological repair project this time, please."

She patted his shoulder, "Of course, Coop. No problem."

Sure.

When the lunch crowd thinned a bit, Cooper wandered into the back kitchen and stood by the window that looked out over the sand and waves. The fog had moved out to sea and formed a grey band on the horizon. It stirred dim feelings that seemed rooted in memories but he couldn't tell which memories. He sighed as he watched the subtle workings of his mind begin to weave a tapestry of sadness. A decade ago he would have seen this feeling as the prelude to depression and he would be trying desperately to hold it back. Today, however, he wasn't concerned. His mind was no longer an enemy, merely a sometimes confused and muddled friend. He turned his attention back to the kitchen and the work he loved.

By the time they had closed the cafe at 4:00 pm and Cooper had done pre-breakfast preparations for the morning, the fog had drifted back in. As he locked the kitchen door and walked around the side garden to the path that wound in a steep slope down to the beach, he allowed himself to become aware of the melancholy that had been building ever since Connie's "lost young man" had left the cafe.

He thought about his own arrival in Carson Beach. He had spent over twelve years in a semi-monastic existence at a Taoist retreat center located in the Cascade Mountains near McCloud, California. Restlessness, grief, and loneliness brought him to the Turning Wheel Taoist Center over twenty years ago. Within its gentle discipline he gradually found healing, contentment, and community. His decision to leave was reached after several months of dialogue with Andy and the others. It had become time for him to reenter a broader experience of life and he was curious about what he might be able to see and do. Andy had a good friend in Carson Beach, Oregon, named Connie Delaney who would be delighted to offer Cooper a job as cook in her cafe. Connie's partner, Mary O'Hara, had been to the Turning Wheel several times on retreat and Cooper knew her slightly. He wasn't going into the complete unknown. But that day as he drove north on the Interstate he felt as lost as ever a grown man could feel.

In the ten years since that day he had established a new home and was now the owner/cook of the Happy Frog Cafe. The little boy inside of him was still vulnerable and would occasionally pay a visit when a sight, sound, or aroma would remind him of the inescapable existential loneliness that came with being alive. He had become skilled at befriending and comforting this lonely part of his psyche that most people buried, avoided, or shamed into silence. But loneliness remained loneliness and there were times when all his skill and attention was required to maintain balance.

He walked along the beach through the thickening fog about five hundred yards until he came to a break in the cliff face and a path the led back up to the street. Once inside his cottage he acknowledged to himself that he was content to be sad and lonely this evening. He went around the cottage and turned on all the lights. Usually he preferred to let the place become a cozy den in the evening, lit only by several oil lamps he had picked up at a second hand store down at the waterfront, but this evening he intended to be kind and patient with the young part of himself who was shrinking from the growing dimness and who shivered in the damp evening.

He arranged his small futon and pillows close enough to the wood stove to feel the warmth and pulled the reading lamp up beside him. The fire had been damped during the day and needed only a bit of kindling to return to life. Over the past few years he had become skilled at the delicate balance required to keep a wood stove from overwhelming the room with heat. He spent a few moments with his handwritten journal, then knelt by the small bookshelf in the corner that contained a mixture of library and personal books, chose one, and placed it on the floor beside the futon.

Cooper's Journal

A young man stepped into the Frog this morning, and I have the feeling he has stepped into my life as well. Connie's eyes had that other worldly look when she told me he was looking for a home and that I needed to talk with him. After ten years I still don't understand Connie's fey gifts; whether she is simply ultra intuitive or actually intertwines with another space and time. I'd like to think that the Cosmos is mysterious enough that such could happen, but I still have a deeply conditioned mental process that likes to call itself, "rational." Sometime I think it doth protest too much, fearful that it will lose control and that a Bigger World than it can stand will engulf it - that a powerful dark wave will sweep away its illusions of predictability and leave it floating in a chaotic ocean. Well, I'm already bobbing around in that ocean and predictability is just a myth to which I sometimes cling purely out of habit.

Watching the fog settle its evening blanket onto Cliff Street, I feel the familiar disquieting loneliness begin to insinuate itself into the comfortable solitude. A mysterious and obviously lonely young man arrives and I feel myself identifying with him. I project my own younger self onto him and my mind opens to the lost emotions of my memories. When Paulette died I became an abandoned child, bereft, stranded on a island, yet surrounded by strangers whose well-meaning presence only exacerbated the loneliness.

Connie's right. I need to talk more with that young man from the cafe. I also need to befriend a young man within my own psyche this evening.

Cooper heated a bit of cooking oil in a large pan and added a half cup of Oroville Redenbacher gourmet popcorn. He stood by the gas stove, gently shaking the pan and listening to the comforting sound of the popping corn inside. When the popping was finished he melted some butter in a sauce pan and poured it over the popcorn. He added some salt then reached to the top shelf and took down the big pottery bowl and dumped the buttered, salted popcorn into it. He stirred it with a long wooden spoon until it was mixed well and set it down on the floor beside the book. He opened a bottle of Rogue Amber Ale and poured it into a glass, *Some popcorn for the child inside, some ale for the adult, and we're all set for the evening.*

He sat on the futon and leaned against the comfortable arrangement of pillows, letting his feet stretch out. He took a sip of beer and smiled to give some sense of comfort to that young frightened part of himself. He sampled the popcorn and smiled again. Then he opened the book and began to read aloud, "The Mole had been working very hard all morning, spring cleaning his little home…"

Reading the cozy adventures of Mole, Rat, Badger, Otter, and Toad aloud brought a feeling of comfort and tenderness to his spirit. The younger, sadder parts of his psyche drifted into the background, feeling cared for and protected. After about a half hour of listening to his own voice, Cooper gently closed *The Wind in the Willows* and put it back on the shelf. He cleaned up the popcorn dishes and damped down the fire. The intense lonely feelings had given way to a comfortable melancholy. Life was just what it was, filled with pleasure, pain, gain and loss. He had experienced enough of the comings and goings in his life not to fall prey to the dramatic stories that contaminated so much of the cultural collective consciousness. *If I want stories,* he said to himself, *I'll get them from carefully selected sources. Ratty and Mole, for instance.*

He took a container of left over clam chowder from the refrigerator, poured it into a sauce pan and set it on the stove over a low flame. He poured a small glass of Willamette Chardonnay and took it over to the low table by the window that faced Cliff Street. The fog blanket had isolated a section of the street as if it were removed from the world; beginning a block to the right and ending a block to the left. Outside these boundaries there might be nothing real in existence. *Maybe nothing ever exists outside my perception,* Cooper mused.

He selected another book from the shelf, poured the chowder into a bowl, and sat at the table. Usually he didn't read while eating, but this evening it was important not to leave his mind entirely to its own devices. He opened the copy of Tan Twan Eng's, *The Gift of Rain,* he had picked up at the county library and was immediately drawn into the complex story. For the next hour the world of the book intermingled in his experience with the warmth of the chowder and cool tang of the wine.

Having nourished both the adult and the child, he cleaned up the dishes and then did some evening Qigong movements, gentle breathing and stretching designed to facilitate relaxation and sleep. As he arranged his bedding for the night, he was aware of the memories of Paulette which usually came at this time of the evening. Allowing these memories to drift into his consciousness enabled him to avoid the unconscious strain that comes from repression that often masquerades as letting go. He smiled at the memories, then let them slip away without grabbing them and working them over in his mind. Then a more recent memory emerged, that of sharing tea with Ito at the teahouse in Ito's beautiful garden. He took a deep breath and laid down, pulling the comforter around him and allowed his mind to gently drift in an open manner, letting thoughts flow out as quickly as they flowed in. Some days were more difficult than others. But sleep comes naturally if it is not resisted.

I'll have to talk to that young man, he thought as sleep gently slipped in.

Chapter 3 - What Were Their Names?

Breakfast was Cooper's favorite meal and he wanted those who were breakfast guests at *The Happy Frog* to enjoy it as much as he did. He was in the kitchen by 4:30 on weekday mornings. The darkness of the morning was transformed by the warmth of the oven, the glow of the working lights, and the aroma of coffee, oatmeal, and biscuits. Everything came to life, not abruptly and shatteringly, but slowly and gently, giving the body and mind time to adapt to the movement from unconsciousness to consciousness; from the dreams of the night to the different dreams of the day. This was the way Cooper's days began and he enjoyed creating an atmosphere where it might begin that way for his guests as well.

This morning his own mood was slow to come along. His sleep had been interrupted by restless dreams and intervals of wakefulness fueled by irrational fears vaguely associated with the dreams. He couldn't remember the content of the dreams, nor much of the thoughts that kept him awake. He was familiar with the aftermath however: a mind that saw the world through a glass bleakly, the kind of mind that thought of comets crashing into the Earth, bringing to a futile end the whole useless experiment in human life.

The ordinary things of life once again came to his aid. The taste of coffee accompanied by its wonderful aroma; the sound of the gas flame against the grill; the paint-pot bubbling of the oatmeal - all these worked their magic, bringing him literally to his senses; those of smell, sight, sound, touch, and taste. These embodiments of living were always the salvation for his disembodied soul.

He remembered a conversation from many years ago when he stood in the middle of the monastery kitchen trying to fend off a full-blown panic attack over preparing an afternoon meal for thirty people.

"You're thinking too much about the people you're feeding," Andy said, "think about cooking, not eating."

"But the purpose of cooking is to prepare food for eating, isn't it?" Cooper asked, still holding back the anxiety and panic.

"Then, what is the purpose of eating?" Andy asked.

"Well," Cooper considered, "to provide fuel for the body?"

"What is the purpose of the body?"

"Shit," Cooper thought, "I was all ready to pack my bags and leave the monastery in disgust and disgrace and instead found myself settling in for another 'Zen' talk." He replied, "The body is a vehicle for experiencing life, I suppose."

"Yes," Andy said, "a vehicle for experiencing life. And where is this 'life' that is to be experienced?"

Cooper sensed a glimmer of something in the corner of his mind. "I suppose it is in each moment."

Andy laughed, "I'm sorry to be doing this Zen question/answer thing. It's just that we so easily get seduced by the illusion that the present moment is somehow merely a time of preparation for some future moment, and cooking is a great example of that. Do you see? Cooking is not preparation for eating. Cooking is cooking! When you understand that, being Head Cook is no longer a problem."

For Cooper, being cook at The Happy Frog was not a way of earning a living. It was living itself. While dicing tomatoes, dicing tomatoes was everything. When the sauce was simmering, the aroma was everything. When it was served the presentation was everything. When it was eaten, the eating was everything. Nothing was preparation for something else. Everything was complete in itself.

By the time Connie arrived at the back door at 5:30, ready to begin the morning work of providing service and community for her customers, the cafe was filled with the aroma of fresh coffee, biscuits, and oatmeal. Cooper was just cutting up the potatoes, peppers, onions, rosemary, and basil for their ever-popular rosemary-basil potatoes.

"Morning, Coop," she sang out as she bustled through the kitchen with an armload of freshly laundered table cloths and napkins. "Who's your wager on this fine morning?"

The Happy Frog opened each morning at 6:30. Cooper and Connie would bet on who would be the first customer of the day. If one of them guessed right, the other would handle the garbage and compost duty for that day. If neither was right, that duty was settled by the flip of a coin.

"I'll bet on Cap'n Phil," Cooper said.

"Good choice," Connie replied, "but you'll be wrong. I'm going to bet on Carl."

"Who?" Cooper asked.

"That young man from yesterday."

"Oh," Cooper said softly, remembering his last thoughts before sleep last night. "Connie, if this is one of your fey moments, all bets are off. We agreed to that, remember." At certain times, Connie's hunches were extraordinarily accurate predictions, emerging from an awareness of things unseen and unnoticed by most people.

"Nope," she replied, "It's just sort of wishful thinking. I'd like to think he hasn't run away."

"Hmm," Cooper nodded and began to arrange the potatoes and other ingredients on a large roasting tray.

At 6:30 Connie turned on the cafe lights and unlocked the front door. No one was waiting on the front porch, but just as she returned to the counter, the chime announced the winner of the morning's bet. A short, grey-haired man in a pea coat and fisherman's cap hunched through the door with a gruff greeting.

"Ah," Connie said in her cheerful hostess voice, "Cap'n Phil, top o' the morning to you."

"Humph," snorted the man as he seated himself at the counter.

Connie took down one of the hand crafted mugs from the shelf and set in on the counter in front of the grizzled man. She filled a carafe from the coffee urn and then filled Phil's cup.

"You're out early this morning," she said. "Shall I have Coop fix you a bowl of oatmeal?"

He looked up and grudgingly let his lips curve in a smile. "Sure, Connie, that would be nice. I need something warm and friendly to balance my frozen heart."

"Blather," scolded Connie, "frozen heart indeed!"

Cooper walked out of the kitchen humming a tune and greeted Phil with, "Cap'n Phil, you have saved me from a day of hauling garbage."

"Picked me did you," snorted Phil into his coffee.

"Sure did. Thanks for showing up."

"So, Captain, what's the sea saying today?" Cooper asked

He sighed and gave a rueful smile , "The sea doesn't talk to me anymore, I'm afraid. We seem to be estranged, she and I." He gave another sigh and adjusted himself on the stool, grimacing a bit as he tried to make himself more comfortable.

"Some pain today, Phil?" Cooper asked.

"Damn medications," he snorted, "one makes me dizzy. Another one makes me feel foggy and confused. I don't know if any of them actually help the pain. They just give me other symptoms to worry about besides the pain. Damn, Coop, it is a pisser to get old. Don't let it happen to you."

"That ship's sailed," Cooper smiled while he picked up a pottery bowl and spooned up a steaming helping of multi-grain cereal. He sat the bowl in front of Phil and looked at him. His comment rang true. Phil seemed to be more and more in a haze lately, walking tentatively, as if he were not completely sure where his next step would land. A few days ago Cooper had noticed him standing outside the front door of the Happy Frog, looking around like a man who was lost in an unfamiliar town, a bit frightened to suddenly find himself on an strange street with no memory of how he got there. Then Skip walked by him and opened the door to the cafe, patting him on the shoulder and saying a word of greeting as he passed. Skip stood and held the door. "You going in, Captain?" At that Phil smiled and shook his head, "Thanks, Skip, I'm just heading down to the overlook. Guess I was lost in thought there for a minute." He walked back up the path to the main sidewalk like a man who knew where he was but still not sure what he was doing.

Captain Phil was, in truth, a Captain, USN retired after a 30 year career and like many a retired sailor could not be far from the ocean. But Cooper noticed that he still seemed lost.

Cap'n Phil nodded his head to Cooper. "I had a friend on the Ruben James," he said, "actually my father was on the Ruben James."

Cooper looked at him for a moment, trying to process his comment.

"The song," Phil said, "the song you were humming."

Cooper hadn't realized he had been humming, but the Cap'n got it right. He had been humming "Wildwood Flower," one of his favorite old folk songs, also the tune to the song, "The Good Ruben James," written by Pete Seeger about a destroyer that was the first casualty of WWII, sunk on convoy duty off the coast of Iceland.

Cooper began to sing, *"What were their names, tell me what were their names."* Phil smiled and his gravely voice joined in, *"Did you have a friend on the good Ruben James? Oh, what were their names, tell me what were their names. Did you have a friend on the good Ruben James?"*

They shared a smile. "Your father was actually on that ship?"

"Yep," Phil nodded, "He was one of the forty-four."

Cooper sang another line of the song: *"When that good ship went down, only forty-four were saved"*

"Did he make it through the war?" Cooper asked.

"Yep. Never saw any more action. Spent a couple of years in

Washington, then somehow was always too early or too late for the fun wherever he was."

"Sounds pretty good to me."

"Frustrated him. He wanted action. Back then the Cap'n put the Ruben James between the sub and a big ammo ship. Hadn't been for the Niblack I wouldn't be here drinking this coffee."

"The Niblack?"

"USS Niblack - close enough that night to pick up the survivors. Dad always felt that the U-Boat Captain could have done more damage, but held off to give the rescue time. Don't know about that, but Dad got to meet that U-Boat Captain after the war. Got a picture of the two of them together."

"Quite a story," Cooper said, meaning it.

"That's all I got," Phil shook his head, "stories and more stories. Nobody wants to hear 'em any more."

"What was your father's name, Phil?" Cooper asked.

"James," Phil said, "James Ralph Peterson." He sipped his coffee and looked at Cooper for a moment, then continued. "He spent his life after the war running a hardware store in Boise, Idaho. Worked hard, enjoyed hunting and fishing. Never missed life at sea."

"Not like you," Cooper nodded.

"No, not like me," Phil said softly.

Connie had not been far off in her predictions. The next two breakfast customers were Carson Beach policemen, patrol officers Jim Red Cloud and David Phillips. Following close on their heels came Carl de Wilde, still looking somewhat dazed and lost but perhaps returning to the warmth of the Happy Frog from a half-remembered sense of comfort left over from yesterday.

After getting Jim and David their mugs of coffee, Connie walked over to Carl who remained by the door, unsure where to go next.

"Good Morning, Carl," she said, "how are you?" The silence with which she waited for his response indicated to him that she actually wanted to know.

"Um ... I'm OK," he replied, "but I need to talk with you. You talked about renting me a place but I don't have any money and I don't really know what I'm ..."

"Yes," she nodded, "I understand. But the old thing is just sitting there. It's not much, just a shack, but it's watertight, has a stove and some simple furniture, and a bed. You can have it free for two weeks, then start rent. Think of it as a 'move-in special.'"

"Well," he scratched his head, "thanks, but I don't know how long I'll stay."

Connie remained silent for a moment, smiling gently into his eyes. "Would you like breakfast?"

Carl chuckled, "Yes, I can afford that. My credit card is not quite maxed out yet."

"Sit down wherever you want," she gestured around the cafe. "I'll get you some coffee."

Carl smiled to himself as he went to a small table by the window. *I guess I want coffee.*

Over at the counter Cooper and Cap'n Phil were singing *The Ruben James* together from the beginning while Cooper went about grilling sausage.

It was there in the dark of that uncertain night.
We watched for the U-Boats and we waited for a fight.
Then a whine, and a rock, and a great explosion roared.
They laid the Ruben James on that cold ocean floor.

The singing seemed to lift Phil's mood and when they were finished, he turned to his oatmeal with some relish.

Connie came into the kitchen. "David and Jim want the usual," she said,

"And my young man might want a cheese omelet."

"*Might* want?" Cooper teased, "You don't know for sure?"

"I just don't want to put him off. I think I've come off too strong. Too odd. Too mother-hen."

"It won't hurt to ask him. Might make him more comfortable. Did he ask for the coffee?"

"Well... no," she sighed.

"Hmm... If you're really worried about coming on too strong, why don't I go take his order and you fix the pancakes for our officers."

"Oh, thanks, Coop. That would be great." She turned quickly to the grill.

As Cooper walked out into the cafe he had a sudden realization: *I've been played! Again.*

Cooper stopped by Jim and David's table for a moment. "Streets safe for decent citizens?" he asked.

"Will be when we get back to work," Jim Red Cloud smiled.

"Don't hurry," Cooper said, "give the evil-doers a few moments rest."

"We don't have evil-doers in Carson Beach, only miscreants," laughed Red Cloud, "but don't you worry. We'll take care of them once we finish our pancakes. Hope Connie makes them. Her's taste better than yours."

"Careful, Red Cloud, didn't you learn in the Army not to make the cook mad?" Cooper patted his shoulder and walked to the back of the cafe where Carl sat drinking his coffee. He walked up to Carl's table and sat down opposite him.

"Don't mean to be intrusive," Cooper said, "but I remember seeing you yesterday. My name's Jim Cooper, but everyone calls me Coop." He extended his hand across the table.

Carl shook his hand. "My name's Carl," he said, "Carl de Wilde."

"Hello, Carl, what would you like for breakfast?"

Carl smiled, "I sort of thought Connie decided that for people."

"Only on occasions. Mostly she minds her own business. No, let me take that back. Often..., no, sometimes she minds her own business. This is one of those times. What would you like?"

"You're the cook, aren't you? What would you recommend?"

"An order of Rosemary Potatoes, they're a specialty here, some sausage that comes from a small ranch down the coast, and scrambled eggs."

"Sounds good," Carl agreed.

Cooper got up and headed to the kitchen.

Carl stopped him and said, "Would you mind making that a cheese omelet instead of scrambled?"

Cooper smiled, "No problem," and continued back to the kitchen.

Naturally.

Carl savored his omelet and potatoes, enjoying every bite. The fog had yet to make its way to land and the morning sun played on the whitecaps. He felt a strange sense of comfort he hadn't felt for months. Picking up his mug he walked up to the counter and took an empty stool. "Could I have a refill, please," he asked Cooper who was cleaning the counter during a short pause in customer traffic.

"Of course," Cooper said. "Would you like to try some French Press?"

"Isn't that extra?" Carl asked.

"Only if the owner finds out," Cooper whispered.

"I don't want to get you in trouble," Carl said.

"I'll risk it," Cooper continued to whisper as he ground coffee and spooned it into a press pot. He filled the pot with hot water and stirred it a bit. "Take about four minutes," he said.

"So Carl," Cooper said after the coffee had been poured into Carl's empty mug, "at the risk of sounding snoopy, what brings you to this little cafe on the coast?"

Carl took a sip of the coffee and murmured appreciatively, "Don't have the faintest idea. I just ran away, I guess."

"Ran away, huh?"

"Yeah, I really have no idea where I'm going or what I'm doing."

"Really," Cooper said, "What are you doing right now?"

"Well," Carl hesitated, "I've sort of kicked over the traces. I called off a long engagement. I left my job without notice. I have no income. I don't know what I'm going to do…"

Cooper interjected, "I mean what are you doing right now?"

"I…" Carl stammered, "I'm taking a trip, escaping I guess."

Cooper smiled, "That's probably true, but…what are you doing *right now?*"

"Oh," Carl smiled, "I guess I'm having coffee and talking to you."

"You guess?"

He laughed. "I'm having coffee."

"No guesses?"

"No guesses. I'm definitely having coffee."

"So it would appear," Cooper laughed and went over to the grill to scramble some eggs and dish up some potatoes. He put the hot plates up on the counter where Connie whisked them away. Cooper returned to lean against the counter and asked Carl, "And where is it that you're having this coffee?"

"Where?"

"I asked you."

"Well, here in Carson Beach, I guess."

"Guessing again?"

"Here. Carson Beach"

"And is it OK to be sitting here in Carson Beach having coffee?"

"Well, yeah, but…"

"No 'buts', is sitting here, talking to me, having coffee OK?"

"Well …"

"No 'wells'. Right now, right here, at this particular moment without reference to some past or future moment, things are OK. Is that so?"

"Yes," Carl said with resignation, "but when I have to …"

"Just stick with here, now, and your coffee for a few minutes. I've got some orders to get out. The cafe closes at 4:00 pm. Why don't you come by about 4:30 and I'll show you around town and we can talk about the past and future a bit if you'd like. Or," he thought a moment, "better yet. I have to take an early run to the Corvallis Farmer's Market tomorrow morning. I could use some help. Would you like to come along?"

Carl shrugged his shoulders and took a deep breath, "Might as well… I mean, yes, I'd enjoy that."

"Good, then" Cooper said, "I'll pick you up at about 6." He poured the pressed coffee in Carl's cup and returned to the back kitchen. Connie came in with an order for pancakes and a query. "How's he doing?" she asked.

"OK, woman, you got your way. Once again I'm butting into other people's business where I've got no call. I hope you're satisfied."

"Coop," she protested, "you never, ever, do anything because I want you to. You always do just exactly as you please. You can't fool me."

"No," Cooper sighed and shook his head, "I can't."

Chapter 4 - Who Are These People?

Early Saturday morning, just at nautical twilight, with the horizon barely visible, Cooper pulled his 1991 Jeep Cherokee pickup into the alley behind the old fisherman's cottage that Carl was renting from Connie and Mary. Mary owned several small pieces of property around town, most a legacy from her father who settled in the town when it was a rough and tumble lumber town and fishing village. Each property seemed to serve as a stabilizing place for families or individuals who needed a home, however temporary, in which to find their footing. It didn't surprise him that Connie had seen such a need in Carl. A light was on in the cottage and Carl opened the door as Cooper drove up.

"Morning," Cooper said as Carl opened the door and slid into the passenger bucket seat. He was dressed in jeans and a dark blue Michigan State sweatshirt. "Michigan State, I see."

Carl took a deep breath. "Yes," he said.

Cooper pulled the Cherokee through the alley and turned right toward Highway 101 which ran through the town of Carson Beach, providing a bottleneck of traffic on summer weekends. This early, however, it would be no problem. They were silent as Cooper turned north toward the road that would take them over the foothills into the Willamette Valley and the town of Corvallis.

Making conversation, Cooper asked, "What did you study at Michigan State?"

"I was a fine arts major," Carl said with a tinge of embarrassment in his voice.

"A *fine* arts major? Or a fine *arts* major?"

"Beg pardon?"

"Just early morning humor," Cooper smiled. "Were you fine as an arts major, or just ordinary?"

"Oh," Carl chuckled, "Truthfully, I was ... I was going to say, 'ordinary,' but I graduated with honors and the faculty encouraged me to stay in the field. I'm a painter, mostly - watercolors, oils, acrylics - all the standard mediums. Amy always said I should stop putting myself down about my art."

"Amy?"

Carl hesitated in silence for several minutes. Cooper remained silent as well. Then Carl said, "Amy was my fiancee. We had been engaged over four years and were finally setting the date when I ran out. That was a couple of weeks ago. I just left, bailed on her, on my job, on my life and got in my truck and drove west." He paused and shrugged his shoulders, "and here I am."

"Yes," Cooper nodded, "here you are. No place else to be."

When they reached Newport, the sky was brighter but it would still be a while before the sun came over the coastal mountains. They turned east on Highway 20. Cooper loved the drive from Newport to Corvallis. Much of what is lovely about Oregon could be seen in that fifty mile stretch of road. Pine and fir forests lining the road, keeping the car in and out of shade on the sunniest of days; open rolling spaces supporting vineyards and pastures; the river opening into the Willamette Valley and the University town. Cooper was a Beavers fan. He would have preferred a more aggressive name for the Oregon State athletic teams, but Beavers it was. He also loved the creative atmosphere of Corvallis.

Each Saturday morning and Thursday evening from May through November, a Farmer's Market sprang up along the banks of the Willamette River where it winds through the town park. Cooper loved the Farmer's Market. He was fascinated by the hands and faces that presented the produce at each stall. They communicated the natural weather-beaten beauty of people who know that life arises from the ground and returns to the ground. People who saw each day as a surprise and a bonus, not an assumed prerogative.

The rest of the drive was spent mostly in a companionable silence. Cooper was easy to be with and did not ask probing questions. Carl told him a bit about his life and art and about the dream of "dancing feet" that had supplied the final impetus for his flight westward. Cooper had nodded and seemed delighted to hear the story, but did not pry.

The morning was especially beautiful though still cool as they pulled off the highway and moved toward downtown Corvallis. Saturday was market day for Cooper. Connie took over the Happy Frog and he shopped for supplies. He liked to arrive early to avoid the crowd and to have an opportunity to scout the best of the produce. The early morning sun shone on bundles of Swiss Chard, on carrots that looked as if they actually came from the ground rather than a machine lathe, and on beets that still had soil clinging to them. The colors provided a tableau that settled Carl into a pleasant mood. They walked slowly through a long aisle that stretched along the river park, tables and tents on both sides of them, and Carl let the sounds, smells, and sights wash over him.

They reached the far end of the stalls and turned to wander back down the second aisle, nearer the street, that contained the bakers, coffee vendors, and others offering tasty treats. The aroma of fresh coffee drew them immediately to a booth where a rosy-cheeked woman sat beside a large coffee urn. She smiled and waved a hand in greeting. "Hi, Coop, you're out early today. Who's your friend?"

"Hello, Gloria," Cooper said. "This is Carl de Wilde." Carl appreciated the fact that Cooper simply introduced him without needing to give details designed to assign him to a category. Gloria's round face seemed even more cherubic with the blush the cool air provided her cheeks.

Cooper turned to Carl, "Gloria and Stan operate a coffee shop that has been a campus institution for twenty years, the *Bean Around*. Turning back to

Gloria he said, "I was looking for the new Starbucks that I hear has opened up. Can you direct me to it?"

She lifted herself from her folding chair and punched Cooper's shoulder. "It's not their corporate policy to serve this close to fresh produce. Guess you'll have to settle for a cup of the more modest and unassuming local brew. I hope you're not too disappointed."

Cooper bowed and smiled. "I will make do with whatever you are able to provide. Seriously," he added, "how are things going with the new Starbuck's open?"

"Actually pretty good," she said as she reached into a box beneath the table and took out two mugs rather than the paper cups that were stacked beside the urn and splashed some hot water from a thermos into the mugs to warm them up, "We've noticed a bit of a dip on weekend mornings, but you know, we've never drawn the young professional crowd that much. Our business has always been campus-oriented, students and faculty. They seem to be sticking to habit. We're all for sticking to habit." She swished the hot water around in the cups and poured it on the ground, then drew the dark coffee brew from the urn into them, filling the air with a marvelous aroma.

Cooper handed a steaming cup to Carl and said, "Stan and Gloria get their coffee from the Naked Coffee Company in Lincoln City, the same roasters who supply us at The Happy Frog. "

"It's wonderful," Carl said as he sipped the coffee.

"By the way," Cooper said to Gloria, "Where's Stan this morning?"

"He's home sick, Coop. The poor man is actually down with the flu. Has been for two days now. Feeling a bit better this morning, but I made him stay in bed with hot tea and the promise of a full season of "Foyle's War" DVDs to watch."

"Wonderful. Give him my best and tell him 'Go Beavers!'"

"Go Beavers!" she replied and sank her ample body back into her chair by the heater.

They wandered down the row with their coffee warming both body and spirit. "I don't actually worry about Stan and Gloria." Cooper said. "Certain establishments have such a unique blend of product, service, and atmosphere that no amount of competition, corporate or otherwise, can actually threaten. Stan and Gloria are artisans, people who put their own creative stamp on whatever trade they practice. Despite hard times, or maybe especially in hard times, people who put something extra, something unique and creative, into what might be called 'ordinary' products or services, will do well."

Carl raised his eyebrows. "That sounds good. But…"

"But?"

"Well, I've struggled with being an 'artisan' ever since I left college. I have no money. I'm in debt. I'm clueless as to what comes next."

Cooper nodded, "I think the artisan mindset has to contain an element of modest expectations. An artisan isn't out to conquer the economic world. He or she needs to be content and grateful to be able to provide themselves the basics and beauties of life in a simple and direct manner."

"Do you consider yourself an artisan?" Carl asked.

"Yes, I do," Cooper said without hesitation. "I've reached the point where I consider my daily life as a cook to be my primary art. In a more prosaic sense I also provide the basics of my life by doing that which I am pleased to do for its own sake. Even an artisan, however, can struggle if he or she does not bring the very best of themselves to their art."

Carl pondered as they walked on, *The very best of myself? What might that be, and how do I bring it?*

They continued to walk leisurely through the Market, talking about the difficulty that the artisan faced in contemporary culture. Carl felt his "inner artist" begin to stir after several weeks of silence. He even started to think of unpacking his painting supplies when they returned to Carson Beach.

"We'd better get serious about supplies before the crowd arrives," Cooper said suddenly. "I've been relaxing and forgetting that we're here on a mission."

"A mission?"

"A mission to feed the frog!" Cooper almost shouted. He raised his arm and pointed back to the stalls of produce. "We must be off!" he cried, "We must enter the world of produce and produce a harvest for our small cafe. Quickly, my friend!" He laughed and walked briskly back up the row of farmers. Carl smiled and shook his head, then set off to catch up with his friend. *Yes*, he thought, *maybe a friend*.

Cooper stopped at a large collection of tables which displayed a colorful array of carrots, beets, leafy greens, potatoes, onions, broccoli, and assorted things for which Carl had no name whatsoever.

"Hello Cora," he said to the lean weathered woman standing behind a set of scales.

"Howdy, Coop," the woman said , allowing a slight upward curve of the right corner of her mouth indicate pleasure at seeing Cooper. "How's it hanging?"

"Low and ripe," Cooper replied, "How's your own fruit?"

"Long gone," she said, the corner of her lips turning up just a bit more.

Cooper and Carl spent the next thirty minutes selecting produce, boxing it up, and carrying it to Cooper's Cherokee. When they were finished, Carl stood looking at the array of edibles in the pickup bed, taken with their variety, color, and texture. "This is quite a sight for a man whose experience of food has been primarily Kruger's."

Cooper nodded, "It took me several years to acclimatize myself to real food and how to cook it."

"Where did you learn to cook?"

"I'll tell you that story over some more coffee. Let's walk over to the *Bean Around* - that's Gloria and Stan's place. It's only a few blocks from here, toward the campus."

"Will the produce be safe?"

"Sure."

As they started to walk from the Market toward town, Cooper's attention was caught by a familiar voice calling, "Cooper-san, *konichiwa*, so nice to see you,"

Cooper was surprised and delighted to hear the familiar voice. He turned and saw Ito, Kathleen, and Sachiko walking toward him. Cooper thought the Ito family were still in Japan. Ito's father had been very sick and the whole family had been staying with him for the past several weeks. "Ito-san," Cooper smiled and hurried over to them. He hugged Kathleen and Sachiko, then rubbed Ito's shoulders in affection. "I'm glad to see that you're back. How is everything?"

Ito shrugged his shoulders and smiled, "Ah, James, you know - everything passes. My *Otousan* has gone and now there is no one between me and the void."

He spoke with philosophical acceptance at the passing of his father. Cooper knew their relationship had been strained but suffused with a sense of honor and love that gave a stability beneath the difficulties. His father had hoped Ito would return to Japan, take a nice Japanese bride, and settle down to take his proper place with his family. Instead Ito married an red-haired Irish lapsed Catholic turned Buddhist, settled into a medical practice in the United States, and left the family obligations to his four brothers and two sisters who remained in Japan. But during his father's last illness Ito had returned to Japan along with Kathleen and Sachiko. His occasional emails over the past months had indicated that the presence of Kathleen and Sachiko had softened his father's ire a bit.

"I'm sorry, my friend," Cooper put his hands on Ito's shoulders, "I'm also naked before that void, as are many of our friends. We aren't really alone, you know."

"Thanks, Coop, I know. I'm fine. It was just a tiring trip. We've only been back a couple of days and just starting to get over the jet lag. Boy," he said looking around at the sunlit displays, "what a wonderful morning for getting back into the comfort of home and friends. How great to see you here, but then I sort of figured you would be. Kathleen said we should call you last night, but I told her you'd be here."

Ito had the remarkable ability to move seamlessly from a formal Japanese persona to the most down-home good old boy American one could imagine, all in the space of two sentences. Cooper sometimes couldn't keep up with the shifts, but then Ito never needed him to.

Cooper turned to Sachiko, a young woman whose hair and face combined her Irish-Japanese heritage in the most appealing ways. Her eyes sparkled with Irish charm one moment, then turned demure and mysterious the next. Any young man who dared a relationship with her would face a challenge as formidable as the quests of Arthur's Knights.

"Sachiko, are you here to stay a while, or are you heading back to the farm?"

"I'm just here for a few days, Cooper-san. I've been away too long. The gang has had their hands full. Crops are magnificent this summer, but there's loads of work to do getting stuff to markets and co-ops."

Sachiko Ito lived on a Community Supported Agriculture farm in the north of Washington, near the Canadian border - a community that had spent the past ten years turning a neglected 20 acres into a model of what might be called "Natural Farming." She had just returned from spending a year on a cooperative farm in Japan under the teaching of the Fukuoka family. Matsunobu Fukuoka was one of the founders of the worldwide sustainable family farm movement that continues to draw many younger people to return to the natural growing of food.

Cooper motioned to Carl who had hung back from the circle of friends, "My friends, I'd like you to meet Carl. Carl is new to Carson Beach. He's a painter, an artist, and he's looking to establish himself and make a new home."

I am? Carl puzzled. *I'm glad you think you know what I'm looking to do. I have no idea myself.*

"Carl, this is Kogan Ito, his wife, Kathleen, and their lovely daughter Sachiko. They are a strange family, Carl. Kogan is a physician, Kathleen is a cop, and Sachiko is a farmer up in Washington state. "

"Nice to meet you," Carl nodded, unsure whether to shake hands, bow, or what.

"Hello," Ito said with a broad grin as he extended his hand and shook Carl's hand warmly. "You really shouldn't associate with a ne'er-do-well like James if you want to make a new home. He is a bad influence."

Carl smiled, "He seems very stable compared to me. I'm really not sure where I'm going to settle or what I'm really doing."

Ito nodded, his lips settling into a small thoughtful smile. "Yes," he said, "that is good. It is when we know what we're doing that we get into the most trouble. It is nice to meet you," he repeated, "perhaps James will bring you to tea some afternoon soon. I will show you the tea house that we built together a year ago. It is simple, but we enjoy it."

Kathleen stepped forward, "Carl, don't let these two overwhelm you, but know that you would be very welcome to visit us. We'd love to get to know you. We love Cooper as a brother and, as they say, 'any friend of his is a friend of ours.'"

The formal yet genuine words of Ito and the warmth and vitality of Kathleen and Sachiko softened one more layer of the fear and confusion that had been encrusting Carl's life. He didn't know what was happening but curiosity was beginning to replace confusion in his mind. *Who are these people? How did I come to suddenly have them surrounding me?*

Chapter 5 - Dancing Feet Again

Carl was struggling to explain himself to a circle of people including Amy, Amy's parents, her sister, and several of her best friends. He couldn't find the right words to counter their accusations. They weren't shouting or attacking but simply shaking their heads in sorrowful disappointment. "You were such a nice young man," Amy's mother was saying, "what on earth possessed you?"

"I don't know!" Carl tried to yell, but the words stuck in his throat and he woke up coughing and gagging. The dim daylight filtered into his room through the curtains along with the steady murmur of the ebb and flow of the waves breaking below on the beach.

I don't know! he thought as he gradually oriented himself to his surroundings. The tiny one-room cottage was still unfamiliar after a week and he continually reminded himself of where he was, and sometimes even who he was. The thought, *What am I doing?* ran through his mind each morning and repeated itself throughout each day. Most of the cues that automatically orient a person to their sense of identity were missing from his life. He had never felt such disorientation, such a sense of being adrift.

His life had been constructed on the foundation of correct behavior and a compliant attitude. Being a "nice boy" had provided him with a secure and warm childhood. His father was the manager of the Holland, Michigan, branch of the People's Bank. The family - father, mother, and older sister, were life-long members of Third Reformed Church. Life was as solid and stable as the old bank building on Main Street where his father spent his days dressed in suit and tie and sitting behind an enormous desk. Sunday school and youth group taught him the rules and provided the right sort of friends.

The wheels began to wobble in East Lansing. Michigan State was not his family's choice of universities. "What's wrong with Hope College?" his father demanded. "It's right here in Holland. It's a good Christian school. You could live at home and save money. Why do you want to go to a big secular university. You'll lose your way, I tell you. You'll lose your way.

"And where," he continued, "did this idiotic idea of studying art come from? Art is fine as an occasional hobby, but studying it? Give me a break."

At his first class in printmaking in his freshman year he sat at a table waiting for the instructor to arrive. Each table had two work stations and Carl was hoping the stool next to him would remain vacant and he wouldn't have to have his work seen by another student. But a tall red-haired girl flung her folio case onto the table and sat down with a sigh. She gave him a small smile and said, "I'm Maggie. Let's make art," and Carl plunged into four years of art, intellectual stimulus, radical ideas, and sexual initiation - all under the tutelage of Maggie Thomas - a free spirit and gifted sculptress from the Detroit suburbs.

Carl's spirit never quite found the freedom that Maggie enjoyed and, just before graduation, she informed him that, although their relationship had been wonderful, she was going off to Paris to study and that it was time for him to move on with his life.

Instead of moving on, Carl moved back; first to Holland to nurse his ego, then to Grand Rapids to teach, have a relationship with Amy, and in general try to go back to the correctness and compliancy that had provided him safety and protection from risk and heartbreak. Amy was safe. Teaching at a Christian High School was safe. Planning for marriage was safe. Then came the dreams of the dancing feet and his whole life began to seem a waking dream; a dream that was now unfolding in an odd little beach town in Oregon.

The cottage/shack he was renting from Connie was quaint to say the least. One room contained a galley kitchen, table and chairs, and a love seat hide-a-bed. A tiny bathroom with toilet, sink and shower occupied one corner of the room, partitioned off by two walls that didn't quite reach the ceiling. Nevertheless, he was grateful for Connie's kindness because his traveling money was exhausted and his bank account back in Grand Rapids would not be of much help. His Visa Card was not yet maxed out, but was on its last legs. He sat on the edge of the sagging sofa bed and looked at his bare feet resting on an ancient rag rug. *Yes*, he thought suddenly, *I had the dream again last night. The dancing feet.*

The memory of the dream flooded to his consciousness. This time the feet danced to an even faster tune than before. The music had a wilder quality and his view of the dancer had shifted to include the legs and waist, clad in a flowing white robe.

Why was this dream special? What distinguished it from the usual? What gave it that feeling more akin to a vision, whatever that was, than to an ordinary dream.?

A coffee brewer sat on the counter alongside a grinder and a canister of coffee beans Connie had supplied. He pulled on a pair of sweat pants and sweat shirt that were hanging on the sofa arm and scooped some beans into the grinder. He filled the brewer with water, ground the beans for a bit, put them into the reusable filter, and pushed the brew button. *Well*, he thought, *I've been here a week. Now what?*

The options were at least beginning to clarify themselves in his mind. Option one was to use what little cash and credit remained and travel back to Grand Rapids. Once there, he could either beg Amy's forgiveness or not, but at least he might be able to return to his job at the school when the fall term began. Option two was actually characterized in his mind as, "not option one." If he wasn't going to return to Grand Rapids in shame, he would be, well... somewhere else. That somewhere else could be anywhere in the country, but right now, here in Carson Beach was where it was.

The coffee maker signaled and he poured a large ceramic mug full, pulled on his socks and shoes and stepped out the door onto the small alley.

He walked a few paces down the alley to where it joined the street, then turned left and walked toward the small trail that cut between two houses down the cliff to the beach.

Carefully making his way down the short path without spilling his coffee, he came to a scattering of large rocks resting against the bluff where the sand began. He sat and sipped the coffee, now cool enough to drink comfortably, and looked out onto the beach and surf. Caffeine began to work its magic on his brain function and, with a sigh, he realized that, for now, this was it. He had never heard of Carson Beach, Oregon, until his westward journey had dumped him onto Highway 101 and a left turn south through Newport took him to a wayside motel and an odd little cafe called The Happy Frog. For whatever reason, this was where he would have to remain for the time being.

As he gazed at the beach, somewhat hazy through the morning fog, he saw a family - father, mother, and daughter, walking along the water's edge. The little girl was no more than five or six years old and was skipping happily through the wet sand in her bare feet. Like all little girls, before self-consciousness squeezes the impulse out of them, she twirled in a happy little dance, splashing the water as she spun.

As Carl watched her, he felt a gradual tide of warmth begin in his tailbone and slowly rise up his spine into his chest. He took a deep breath and let the feeling spread. It was not an alarming feeling. It was comfortable and reassuring. The bare feet of the little girl moving in her morning dance were not the feet of his dream, but they were a pointer; an unexplainable confirmation of whatever energy, or insanity, had propelled him to this spot.

Well, I need a job. I need a permanent place to live. And, he concluded, *I need some breakfast.*

He drank the last of his coffee. After another moment he stood and climbed back up the path to the street. He stood for a moment, looking back toward his shack, then turned in the other direction and walked down the street toward The Happy Frog.

Mary O'Hara had settled comfortably into her early 50s, retaining the fair skin and freckles of her Irish heritage. She sported the same luxurious red hair as her sister, Kathleen, who was married to Kogan Ito. Mary had never been in doubt as to her sexual identity nor her love for Connie, whom she met while they were both attending the University of Oregon in Eugene. Her no-nonsense rationality provided a counterpoint to Connie's fey proclivities while Connie's sense of Celtic magic touched Mary's own hidden Irish mysticism.

Neither was particularly militant for gay and lesbian causes. They had been together for twenty-five years now and lived in the security of their love without any need to explain, justify, or convince others of anything. As a result, few thought about their relationship beyond enjoying them as interesting and friendly people.

Depending on her schedule at the Wildlife Refuge, Mary sometimes helped Connie and Cooper with the early breakfast preparations. This particular morning she and Connie had actually arrived downstairs and started work before Cooper appeared. The work was finished with time to spare and now Mary, Connie, and Cooper were sitting in the kitchen of The Happy Frog, relaxing over fresh brewed coffee.

"How was your trip to the Farmer's Market with that young man?" Mary asked Cooper.

"His name is Carl, honey," Connie reminded her.

"Yes, Carl. Did he enjoy the Market?" Mary continued.

Cooper sipped his coffee and thought for a moment, "I think he's still in a bit of shock. We did meet Ito and Kathleen, just back from Japan. Have you talked to Kathleen since they've been back?"

Mary hesitated, "We touched base for a bit, but I think the trip was rough on them."

"They seemed happy when I saw them, glad to be home," Cooper said.

"Yes, relieved, I think," Mary ventured, "but there was something in Kathleen's voice when we spoke over the phone that was reserved. Kathleen is seldom reserved."

"Tell me about it," Cooper and Connie exclaimed in unison.

Mary continued, "She's been with Kogan long enough now that I think she's picking up some of the Japanese inscrutability."

"Ito can be inscrutable," Cooper agreed, "Sometimes he seems more American than any of us, but that is also part of the inscrutability. Anyway, they invited Carl and me over for tea sometime soon."

Connie put down her mug and said softly, "That would be good for Carl. I think you should take them up on it soon."

Mary and Cooper looked at Connie for a moment, then Mary asked, "Is that a suggestion or one of your 'insights?'" Mary had lived with Connie long enough to view the somewhat fey side of her with less rational skepticism than she felt when they first met.

"It would just be good to do," Connie smiled as she got up. "I'll go open the front door. Time for us to get to work."

Mary stood as well, "Yes, off to the animals I go." She gave Connie a quick kiss, picked up her canvass tote and strode to the back door. Cooper remained seated for a moment, remembering his trip to Japan with Kogan Ito back during the summer break between their graduation from Berkeley and the stress of medical school for Ito and law school for Cooper.

They stayed a week with Ito's parents who lived in on Sado Island, off the coast of Honshu in the Sea of Japan. Together they had attended a performance of the Ondekoza - "Demon Drum Group." The cadre of performers lived as a community on the island, integrating a rigorous regimen of long distance running with hours of practice with traditional Japanese instruments and drums.

The audience sat on cushions on the floor of a school auditorium. The stage was slightly elevated but the overall atmosphere was intimate. Cooper's thoughts were still scattered from the trip and the culture shock of rural Japan. The lights went down and the curtain parted to reveal a huge drum sitting on a stand.

A man walked from the wings and took his place in front of the drum. Cooper had never seen such an archetype of the Masculine as he saw that night in this older man, probably in his late fifties or early sixties, but who could know? The man was dressed in silky flowing pants and a white headband. He was muscular but not in the body-builder, ego-conscious, oily-skin sort of way. His muscles were those of a wild animal, perfectly toned and shaped for the work of being that particular animal - wiry, supple, and spring-like in their tension and release.

The man stood in front of the huge Daiko drum - the monster drum whose chamber was six feet in length and whose leather-covered head was four feet in diameter. He remained motionless for several moments then raised the two drum sticks - wooden dowels a couple of inches in diameter and a foot long - and shouted something that sounded like a warning, or a war cry. Then he raised the sticks even higher and brought them down on the drum head with a thud-thud that shook the air in the hall. He shouted again and again raised the sticks and brought them down, hard! Thud-thud! Then another shout and the driving rhythm of the "O-Daiko" began. Gradually other drummers with various drums began to join.

Every thought in Cooper's mind vanished. All fatigue over the long trip, all the fears of the future that had been his companions for the last year - everything was gone. There was only the drumming. Cooper tried to get a mental handle on what was happening, to regain some sense of the self that the thinking process keeps in place, but he couldn't. There was, for this moment, no self, no-thing that stood between him and the immediate experience of Life. Life, at this moment, was only the drum, the drummer, and the vibration that echoed in Cooper's very bones. He could feel it in his jaw and in his feet, though he had no real sense of "someone" who had a jaw or feet.

Later that evening, as he lay in his room listening to the cicadas fill the night with their own drumming, his "self" returned along with the stream of mental activity that he had learned to call "thought." His mind had been "thinking" all along, but thinking only those "first thoughts" of a living animal - processing stimuli, following a path, noticing everything but fastening to nothing particular. Now "he" was back. "He" wasn't at all sure this was a good thing. The drumming had taken over his life from the internal committees of timid little men who had, up to now, defined it for him, and returned it to Someone far more vital and alive.

"Coop, we have customers," came Connie's lilting voice, waking his from the reverie.

"Yes, I'm coming," he said as he stood up and walked up to the grill, the drumming remaining in his mind.

"He's here," Connie whispered as she stood by the counter.

"Who's here," Cooper frowned.

"The young man, Carl, of course," she smiled.

Of course, he thought.

Chapter 6 - Tea House

Carl, Kogan and Kathleen Ito, and Cooper sat at a low table in the tea house Ito and Cooper had built last year in back of the house where Kogan and Kathleen lived. The tea had been served in a simple manner, echoing the traditional Chanoyu ceremony but with less formality. As the ceremony's name implied, it was simply, "Let's boil water and have some tea."

Carl was initially hesitant about accepting the invitation. Cooper had finally persuaded him by reminding him that Connie thought it would be a good idea. If Connie "suggested" it, who were they to say otherwise? He still felt disoriented and somewhat lost. He knew he was avoiding the unfinished issues waiting back in Grand Rapids, but he continued to take steps that seemed to relentlessly imply that Carson Beach was "home," at least for now.

The small tea house was warm and aromatic with the scent of tea and Jasmine. Sweet cookies and tart pickled vegetables sparked their taste buds as the conversation began with an assumed intimacy that reached out to enfold Carl despite his misgivings. It was one more place that seemed oddly like home.

Kogan Ito and Cooper had been friends since their University days in Berkeley where Ito was a pre-med student and Cooper studied law at Bolt Hall. Ito was a man of two worlds; as western as the Rocky Mountains yet as Japanese as a sixteenth century samurai sword. He could drink beer at the Brass Ass, roar with laughter at the latest lawyer jokes, argue the fine points of Oregon State football, and hint broadly at sexual experiences that Cooper could only dream of. He could also sit in meditation with the stillness and stability of a mountain, wield a sword with fearsome expertise, move a black-inked brush with effortless grace to create exquisite calligraphy, and present a cup of tea in a manner that would make a person feel gratitude merely for being alive.

A year ago, Ito and Cooper built this tea house on the Ito's property. It was a do-it-yourself task that they designed as they went along. They struggled their way through false starts, cleaned up disasters, drank lots of sake and laughed most of the time. The result was a small sanctuary tucked amidst bamboo, ferns, pines, and other flora. A stone paved path led from the back door of the Ito's home and wound only about thirty yards to the tea house, yet led to a place where the main house was not visible and only the forest and tea house seemed to exist.

They didn't know all the needed skills and techniques of carpentry and design when they started, but they knew what they wanted to feel and to experience when they entered the finished house for tea. Cooper knew that there was no substitute for a "design-it-yourself" and "build-it-yourself" approach. The parameters of the traditional tea house served as a flexible guide, but the house was their own, not a copy of the classic Japanese model.

Cooper reflected as they labored that his own life was much the same. He had always known how he wanted his life to feel. With that knowledge, he had been able to build it one board at a time. Sometimes he had to rip out whole walls, and once the foundation crumbled beneath him and had to be redone. He had made some whopper mistakes and was saved from other mistakes by the well-placed help and advice from friends. Gentle words of warning - "You might want to think about that..." saved him worlds of suffering. Other, less gentle advice - "Are you nuts? Get a job, for god's sake!" he was able to ignore. Overall, the life he had constructed was lovely to his mind. It's weather-worn, wabi-sabi walls pleased him. It didn't look like more conventional lives, but for him it was as welcoming a place as Ito's wonderful tea house.

"Quite a move you made, Carl," Kathleen said, "Courageous I would say."

"I don't know," Carl responded, "Calling off my engagement and taking off like I did, I sometimes feel like a little boy who has impulsively run away from home and doesn't know what to do without mother to take care of him."

"Wow," said Kathleen, "if your fiancee was a mother figure you may not have run far enough yet. Run, Forest, run!" she emoted the classic line from Forest Gump.

Carl laughed, then took a sip of his tea to cover his discomfort at the sudden realization that, yes, Amy was "mother" in many ways. He thought of her, of Grand Rapids, of his teaching position at the High School, of his family - and began to feel smothered and confined. He coughed to clear his head a moment and took a couple of deep breaths.

Kathleen leaned forward, her eyebrows furrowed in concern, "Carl, I didn't mean to make you uncomfortable. Please forgive me. I was flip and rude and I ..."

Carl shook his head, "No, no Kathleen, you were right on." He smiled as his throat loosened and his breathing deepened, "I just all of a sudden felt the reality of the claustrophobia of my life back there. I couldn't breathe."

"Still," Kathleen continued, "I shouldn't have been so flip."

Everyone was silent as the atmosphere of the tea house soothed the conversation. It truly was a place where truth could be spoken kindly and with compassion.

Ito spoke softly, "I know the feeling, Carl. I think about going back to Japan to the duties and obligations my siblings want me to assume as the oldest, and I have the same choking feeling. It really is claustrophobic."

Cooper sipped his tea and considered his old friend, then spoke, "Are you going back to Japan, Kogan?"

There was another silence, broken only by Kathleen's sharp intake of breath.

"We're thinking about it," he said, his face looking older and more tired than it did a few moments ago.

"Do you want to move back to Japan?" Cooper asked.

"No, honestly, I don't. It's a sense of duty to my family that is the real pressure I feel. No -" he continued, "Japan is not the place I want to practice medicine. There would be no escape from the pressure of assembly-line medicine; no ability to take a hour with a patient. It is hard enough here, but at least here I can live far enough "off the grid" medically speaking, to enjoy my practice."

Kathleen spoke in a soft voice, "I will go if Kogan decides to go, but I don't want to leave my home, my friends, or my work. I've finally established myself in a man's field to the point where I'm taken seriously. That would be hard to give up for a woman's place in Japan, even though the culture is more "western" in some ways than we are." She shrugged and looked at Kogan, "I'm sorry, but western in most of the unhappy ways I think..."

Ito nodded his head, "Kat is right. Urgency, stress, and productivity are the norm. I don't want to go back to that, but..."

"But?" Cooper said.

"My sister is applying quite a bit of pressure," he signed and smiled at Cooper, "she dominates the family to a degree."

Carl and Kathleen remained quiet.

Ito stretched his back and adjusted his posture on the cushion and continued, "I was born in San Francisco but my parents moved back to Japan when I was about thirteen. I went with them and entered a special program to prepare me for returning to the University of California to study medicine. The plan was for me to get my medical degree and return to make my parent's proud. But I met some bad influences while at Berkeley," he laughed, looking fondly at Cooper.

"Medical school was a great disappointment to me. I could handle the pressure well enough, but the prevailing view of medicine was rational, pragmatic, and cold. Despite being Japanese, I am not as rational and pragmatic as my parent's could wish."

He turned to Kathleen, "I don't know about cold. Am I cold, Kat?"

She leaned toward him and whispered something in his ear.

"No," he smiled, "I would say I'm not cold."

Kathleen leaned her head on his shoulder, "Kogan met me when we were both visiting a retreat center in Northern California," she nodded toward Cooper, "a place Coop landed a few years later. I was an aggressive red-haired hussy and I bewitched him. He didn't have a chance."

Ito laughed, "I didn't. The Irish witch plus the enchanted environment left me no choice."

Carl, fending off a feeling of shyness, took a deep breath and spoke, "You both seem very happy here."

Ito reached across the table and poured more tea in Carl's ceramic cup. "Yes, Carl-san, we are very happy. Although I'm not sure just what 'happiness' might actually be." He turned to Cooper and smiled, "You, Cooper-san, are a happy man. Tell me what happiness is."

Cooper smiled, "You can't bait me, you old samurai. You know as well as I do that to try to find a reason for happiness is to have it slip away. We have to be happy for no reason whatsoever. Happiness is what's there when all our conditioned thinking and compulsive habits slip away. It's the baseline condition of life. We cover it up with chaotic activity and the pursuit of illusions we are told will make us happy. Our very pursuit of it makes it impossible to find."

Ito laughed and said, "Stop thinking and end your troubles, right?"

"A wise sage once said something very like that," Cooper nodded.

Another companionable silence descended on the room. Carl noticed that no one seemed to need to beat a subject to death. Words were spoken, but exchanges stopped before they drifted too far into repetitious opinions. Silence was as important to the conversation as were words. It was a strange setting, yet so very comfortable to him. It was one hundred eighty degrees from the way words seemed to define his life in Michigan. He found that, as the spoken words in the room were relaxed, so too were the workings of his mind. *Maybe,* he thought, *thinking is the problem; or at least a certain kind of thinking.*

More tea was shared. More words were spoken. A quality of contentment settled onto each person present.

Chapter 7 - Good Work

Cooper and Carl sat at a small table on a deck just outside the back door of the cafe and around the corner of the building. It was actually a deck and stairs arrangement connecting with the apartment on the second floor where Connie and Mary lived. Cooper was taking a morning break while Connie handled the kitchen and Karen Wilson, a Williams University student who worked part-time helping out, served customers. Carl had come early for breakfast and Cooper invited him to bring his coffee and sit to watch the surf for a bit.

Cooper sipped from his mug and watched the Brown Pelicans play follow the leader on their way to a day of dive-bombing fish. "You mentioned that you're thinking of staying around for a bit," he said.

Carl followed the Pelicans with his gaze as they flew southwest over the ocean.

"I don't know what else to do," he said softly.

"What do you want to do?" Cooper asked.

"What do I want to do, or what I should I do?" Carl asked in reply.

"I don't think much about what people should do," Cooper said, "there are so many versions floating around of what a person should do that it's too confusing to warrant much thought. What people want to do - now, that's a more interesting exploration."

They both continued drinking their coffee and watching the waves. The sound of the gulls and the rising and falling white noise of the surf allowed a person to be quiet without feeling the need to fill the space with words.

Carl broke the silence, "I'll need a job, I guess."

"Hmm," Cooper nodded, "Do you need a job, or work to do that will help you feed, clothe, and shelter yourself while you go about creating and enjoying your your life?"

"They pretty much go together, don't they?"

"Sometimes they do," Cooper agreed, "but not often. Depends on how you want to spend your time, I guess. You're an artist, aren't you?"

"Well, I taught a couple of classes in art back in Michigan," he paused, "I've sold a few paintings and I majored in art at the University. I'm not sure I'd say I was an artist."

Cooper raised his eyebrows.

"Well," Carl continued, "not a *real* artist."

Cooper kept his eyebrows raised and cocked his head to the right.

"I mean," Carl stammered, "not a successful artist."

Cooper sighed, "Carl, you know, for the last minute I think I've been talking to some peculiar combination of your parents, teachers, and ex-girlfriends - not to you."

Carl shrugged. He did not sense any meanness or rudeness in Cooper's comment, but there was an edge that sliced through his habitual persona, causing him to quickly seal off the slight psychic wound just a bit. Then the confusion and fear would not stay down and he blurted out, "Shit, I don't know. My night times are as different from my day times as, well, as night and day. I woke about 2:00 AM this morning and felt just like a very young child who was homesick, afraid, and totally unable to take care of himself. By the time I got here for breakfast I felt like an adult who would somehow figure this whole thing out. Both parts of me seem completely real at the time."

Cooper laughed, "Oh boy, do I know those two parts. I often wake in the middle of the night terrified and vulnerable, lost, alone, incompetent. Like you, I come to my senses as I wake into the day. I think we're always more vulnerable at night - partly biorhythms and partly childhood training.

"Also," Cooper continued, "bedtime eliminates the distractions and activities that keep those young voices in the background. The mind relaxes and the habitual patterns of childhood appear."

"How do you deal with it?" Carl asked, feeling a current of reassurance gently tingle in his stomach.

"Compassion," Cooper said, "compassion and familiarity with the process. Also, I've learned over the years not to take my conditioned thoughts seriously."

Cooper then changed the subject, "Did you bring some of your art with you?"

Carl returned his attention to the moment, "No," he replied, then added, "I did bring my paint supplies along."

"So," Cooper said, "you plan to paint."

Carl let his irritation slip into his voice, "I haven't planned anything for three weeks!"

Cooper nodded and took another drink of coffee. Then he stood up and said, "Planning is overrated anyway. I have to get back to work. Feel free to just sit here for awhile. Then check with me before you go. I have a phone number I want to give you."

Carl sat on the patio and let his thoughts settle down and meander. He didn't like any kind of confrontation and he was especially uncomfortable when a comment touched the tender spots, places in his life that he tried not to notice. Yet, there was something about Cooper that was accepting and open, even when his words pushed a bit. There was also something about the surf that made it more comfortable to be confused and without direction. A deeper, more consistent rhythm seemed to insinuate itself into his being. Part of his mind continued to send frantic messages about failure and irresponsibility, but the sound of the waves dampened those messages' intensity just a bit.

After a while he brought his cup back around to the front door of the cafe and took it to the counter. Cooper looked up from the grill and motioned to Carl to wait just a moment. He came out from around the counter, wiping his hands on a towel. He held out a slip of paper toward

Carl.

"Here's the phone number of Dorothy Waters. She owns a combination gallery/bookstore called Words and Images. It's up on the highway and a couple of blocks south. You can call her, or just drop by. She's looking for some part-time help."

Carl took the paper, nodded his head, sighed, squared his shoulders and grinned at Cooper. "Here we go," he said as he turned and walked to the door.

Cooper thought, *Yep. Here you go.*

The morning fog had lifted and the sun warmed him as Carl walked the steep slope of Dixon Street up to Highway 101, the main commercial street of town. He had wandered over much of the town already, but a shop called *Words and Images* did not stick in his mind. He turned south and was somewhat shocked by the number of automobiles, RVs, and trucks inching their way through town. He walked along the sidewalk as it curved slightly to the east and saw the Words and Images store across the street on the corner where Bay Street crossed on its way to the waterfront. He waited at the light while the stream of traffic continued to flow, then walked across to the shop.

Walking through the front door felt like walking into the library of an English Estate house. Bookshelves stretched from the floor, through a narrow mezzanine that wrapped around three sides of the store, and on to the ceiling two stories up. Open stairs to the mezzanine tucked against the left wall. The bookshelves extended all the way to the back of the store. They were interspersed with alcoves furnished with comfortable seats. Each alcove displayed a small collection of art. There were perhaps ten of these alcoves in all. A small desk and counter stood just inside the door. The desk was crowded with papers, books, and a computer screen.

A dozen or so customers were browsing the shelves or sitting in the alcoves. A large cat presented itself and began to rub against Carl's legs. *Of course there would be a cat,* he thought. As he reached to pet the cat, a woman walked up to him and extended her hand.

"Hello," she said, "I'm Dot Waters. You must be Carl."

I must be Carl? "It sounds like either Cooper or Connie have been talking to you," he smiled as he took her hand.

"Of course," she returned his smile with a knowing wink, "Those Happy Frog people are always aware of things. Even things you wish they weren't," she added with a playful lift of her eyebrows.

She was a slim attractive woman, perhaps in her late thirties, perhaps older. He found that he really had no idea of a woman's age. She was wearing a black one piece shift over a gauzy white blouse. She was tall, perhaps five feet eight or nine. Her eyes were hazel. Her skin was somewhat pale and smooth. Her hair was auburn. And her hand was still holding Carl's. She studied his eyes for a moment, then said, "You're hired."

" I am?" Carl frowned, "Why? What...?"

Dot released Carl's hand and stepped back, her face flustered. "I'm so sorry," she said, "I just sometimes blurt out things and I don't have Connie's sense of what's appropriate. I don't even know if you *want* a job. I just talked to Cooper and..."

Carl interrupted her apology, "Don't be sorry," he said, "things are just happening so fast that I feel as if my whole life is out of control... or," he stopped for a moment, "or maybe it's more like it is actually under control but by something I can't fathom." He chuckled, "What is this job that I'm hired for, anyway?"

Carl, Cooper, and Dorothy Waters, the proprietress of Words and Images, sat in a small alcove of the bookstore-gallery. Dorothy and Carl had just closed the store for the evening, completing Carl's first day of work at the store; a day he had enjoyed more than any in recent memory. The time had passed without effort amidst boxes to unpack, shelves to straighten, art to hang, and general dusting and cleaning along with the occasional turn at the sales counter. Dorothy seemed a gentle and non-demanding boss. She assumed that Carl was an intelligent and competent adult. Carl noticed that ever since he arrived in Carson Beach he had been treated with that same underlying respect. Even Connie's fey "interference" seemed respectful of his dignity.

They sat around a coffee table in a grouping of small but comfortable chairs. On the three walls of the alcove above them several paintings done in the classical Chinese landscape school of brushwork were displayed. Dot had brewed a pot of Jasmine Green tea which sat on the table. It was a restful end to a full day for all three. Dorothy had been somewhat nervous at her impulsive hiring of this young man whom she really did not know, despite Connie and Cooper's recommendation. Carl was still bemused at the sea change in his own life over such a short span of weeks. Cooper was just plain tired after a full shift behind the grill, after which he took a three mile jog along the beach to work our the stiffness his legs felt from hours of standing. Each, as they sipped their tea in companionable silence, was grateful for the presence of the others.

"That was one of the most satisfying days I've had in a long time, Dorothy," Carl said as he leaned back against his chair. "This shop is a wonderful place to be."

"Dot, Carl. Please remember to call me Dot," she smiled.

"Dot, then," Carl nodded.

Cooper had his eyes closed as he sipped his tea. "It is a lovely place, Dot," he said, "You've done a wonderful job in the past few years. I get the impression that people are coming from as far away as Portland just to browse."

"Well, Coop, people come for the ocean mostly," Dot demurred.

Cooper raised his eyebrows in a familiar gesture.

"Oh, all right, " Dot admitted, "Yes, I do know of people who travel quite a ways to visit. The website is keeping me in contact with some good book people; art people too - though not the "artsy-fartsy" types, thank God." She looked at Cooper, "Don't tell me you don't have people traveling just to eat at *The Happy Frog*?"

"Some do," He said, "Carl came over 2,000 miles."

Dot turned to Carl, "Just to eat at The Happy Frog?"

Carl frowned quizzically, "I… guess that might be the case. It's weird. I had no idea where I was going, other than, 'west.' When I got to the ocean, I was standing on Cliff Street by the parking lot and saw the sign that said, 'Welcome Traveler.' 'That's me' I thought. And here I am. Don't ask me to explain it."

"Oh, I wouldn't dare," Dot smiled, "One doesn't explain The Happy Frog. One simply enjoys it for what it is."

"And what is that," Cooper asked.

"Beats me," Dot shook her head, "Magic is a trivial and misleading word. Maybe it's just like its name implies, a 'happy' place."

Carl asked, "Who named it?"

"Connie and Mary did when they opened the place," Cooper said, "Named it after the statue that Mary found at a little studio along the coast many years ago."

"How did you come to be there? You studied law at Berkeley, didn't you. How'd you end up a cook?" Carl asked.

Dot laughed and Cooper shook his head, "Long, long story," he said.

"You may as well begin it," Carl encouraged.

"Well, without going into the whole story, the cook part of it started about, what is it now? Maybe seventeen or so years ago. I had just taken up residence at a monastery-like retreat center in Northern California. I had drifted around a bit before that, trying to regain my balance after a profound loss…"

"Loss?" Carl said.

Cooper shook his head, "That's another story, one for later." He continued, "The retreat center is called The Turning Wheel. It's guided by an ex-Jesuit priest named Andy Taylor. He used to be the Dean of the Jesuit Divinity School in Berkeley but one day he suddenly resigned and moved to a forest cabin his family had owned near McCloud. It included about 100 acres and gradually it became a place for people who didn't seem to fit with organized religion, yet acknowledged some Wonder and Mystery about the Cosmos, to live and visit. Several people built small hermitages and formed a community with Andy as their reluctant, but very skillful, spiritual guide. Ito-san suggested it to me and I wrote Andy, then visited. I stayed for twelve years."

"Twelve years!" Carl exclaimed, "it must have been a special place."

"Oh, it was," Cooper laughed, "but not in the way I expected. For about a month I rested and savored the quiet, the fellowship, and the wonderful meals the Head Cook, Alex, provided. Then one day"...

"You have got to be kidding," Cooper said as he stood up from his chair. He had been having what he thought was a relaxed conversation with Andy, part of a personal session that every resident had with him three times each week. It was usually a time of receiving reassurance, talking over any issues, and letting Andy's soothing clarity continue to instruct him. This time, however, his words were anything but soothing. They were insane!

"Head Cook! I've been here one frigging month. I barely know where the kitchen is!"

"It's right off the dining hall," Andy said. "You've been there. I saw you cutting carrots yesterday. That place where you were cutting carrots; where the big stove is - that's the kitchen."

Cooper began to panic. "Andy, I came here to decompress and find some equanimity. Running a kitchen that serves two meals and an evening snack every day to thirty men and women is not what I call decompressing!" He actually felt tears rising at the prospect.

"Coop, let me be honest with you," Andy said. "When I invited you to come here I knew it was to be Head Cook. I only waited a month because I wanted you to settle in a bit. But make no mistake, cooking is why you're here."

Cooper stood silently, still wide-eyed. Andy continued, "Do you trust me, Coop?"

"Well, I used to," Cooper said, "but in the past few minutes I think you may have had a small brain fart."

"Sit down, Coop," Andy said. Cooper sat.

"Coop, you don't need me as your teacher. You don't need a parental substitute as do many of the younger people here. You don't need a sensei any longer either. You are your own sensei. What you need is an art, a tangible connection with the physical world. You need a place of refuge from your own mind. You don't need hours and hours of meditation. Some, perhaps, will be of benefit but not to the exclusion of a direct engagement with things you can touch, smell, and taste."

"There's plenty of direct engagement in the daily work here," Cooper protested. "The garden, the building, the cleaning…"

Andy cut him off. "You also need to take responsibility for something outside of your comfort zone, Coop. Trust me on this."

Cooper temporized, "Assign me to work in the kitchen for six months. Alex does a wonderful job as Head Cook. He can teach me this 'art of cooking' can't he? Wouldn't that be better?" God, he thought, I'm whining like a baby. Where's this panic coming from?

Andy just sat there with a sympathetic expression, much like a death row chaplain might adopt at certain awful times.

Cooper continued, "I'd make a horrible mess of things. I'm not organized. My mind doesn't go to details…"

Silence.

As Cooper sat there watching Andy's sympathetic but determined face, the sense of peace that had begun to settle in his chest that morning disappeared into the forest mist. He looked out the window and saw the does with their fawns nibbling the grass around the fence. He wondered if he would ever again sit and watch them in relaxed contentment. This was totally unfair, wrong, not at all the way it was supposed to be. He felt that life had once again done a 'Charlie Brown and Lucy' football jerk on him.

"What about Alex?" he asked.

"Alex is going to Seattle," Andy said.

"He's leaving? I thought Alex was here permanently."

"Permanently?" Andy smiled, "Tell me, Coop, what can you possibly point to that is permanent?"

Cooper smiled for the first time that morning and felt a small chuckle arise. "Let me think. I'm sure there's something." His chest eased just a bit. He remembered the words Sam said to Frodo in The Lord of the Rings. "There's nothing for it, Mr Frodo. We're going up Mount Doom so we might as well get started." He shrugged his shoulders. He'd at least make good use of whatever reflective time remained to him. "Well, how much time to I have? When do I start being Head Cook?"

"Tonight."

Chapter 8 - Lieutenant's Day

Kathleen O'Hara Ito pushed open the door to her new office with a sense of relief. She and Kogan had spent the weekend by themselves at a cabin in the Mount Hood Wilderness. They walked in the forest that was beginning to show signs of Autumn. They talked gently of their life, their love, and of the future. They made love in the afternoons. They sat by the fireplace at night and sipped warming drinks, sake for Kathleen and Irish whiskey for Kogan, laughing at the incongruity of their preferences. Without much discussion they arrived at the decision to remain in Oregon and not return to Japan. It was a natural decision for each of them and each felt the warm assurance of the other's support and love.

Kathleen would have gone to Japan if Kogan had felt he needed to return, but as she sat down at her desk and looked through the plexiglass window into the squad room she knew that this was where she wanted to be. This was her work. For all of its dark edges and stress, she brought to it a confident realism that managed to avoid cynicism. She had taken pre-law in college but shifted to Criminal Justice in her senior year. Then the Oregon State Police academy and ten years as a Trooper, then a graduate degree in Psychological Forensics, and now seven years as a Detective at the regional office in Newport. She managed a marriage, raised a child, and constructed a life. Her colleagues wondered how she did it. She did it by living one moment at a time, and only that moment. *One has to be a Buddhist in this job,* she often thought, *Either that, or insane. Some would say there is little difference between the two.*

She was not religious. When asked, and pressed for an answer to the rude and intrusive question, she would respond, "I'm a lapsed Catholic, non-religious Buddhist, atheistic Humanist who believes in magic."

"Lieutenant, got a minute?" Collins poked his head around the open door.

Lieutenant, she thought, *How about that?* "Sure, Steve. Come on in. You're the first person to call me Lieutenant since the promotion. I appreciate it, but it still sounds a little strange."

"Not strange at all," Detective Steve Collins reassured her. "It fits. You should have been behind that desk two years ago. You know the whole squad has seen you in that role no matter what fat ass was sitting in that chair."

"Well," she smiled, "it will still take some getting used to. I'm going to miss getting out of the office. I hope I don't get fat and lazy."

"Unlike the previous occupant of that chair," Collins said in a tone of sarcasm.

"Let it go, Steve," Kathleen shook her head, "No use going there at all, at all."

Kathleen's new rank came with new responsibilities. She was now the Commander of the Newport Regional office of the Oregon State Police. At least her office didn't have to handle dispatch with its daily chaos. That was now coordinated from the Salem office. She was, however, now saddled with all ongoing criminal investigations that fell under OSP jurisdiction, which usually meant anything the Sheriff's Department or local Police could foist off. The Newport OSP office usually had a backlog of messy, high-profile, and usually unsolvable cases. Kathleen loved it.

She had risen through the ranks without the usual rancor that follows a female detective. Her personality neither threatened nor angered most other officers. An exception was her predecessor in the Newport command office. "Curly" Johansen was a mean unhappy man; a corrupt bully no one could ever pin to illegal behavior. He attempted to make Kathleen's life as miserable as he had made most other female patrol officers and detectives, to no avail. She frustrated his every ham-fisted attempt to undermine, embarrass, or disregard her - usually by a fluid sort of non-resistance, what her partner called "psychological Judo."

"If lard ass has any effect on my life, it's only when I allow it," she often said. And seldom did she ever allow it. She did, however, keep her good friend, Jim Starks, in the Salem office apprised of Johansen's every move, confidentially and subtly. She was a beautiful, generous, competent woman but not a woman to play games with. She knew all the rules, especially the ones to break for good reason.

Detective Collins continued leaning against the doorframe of Kathleen's office. He truly enjoyed seeing her behind that desk. He had healthy respect for her ability. He also had a healthy crush on her - healthy in the sense that both he and Kathleen were happily married and therefore safe to enjoy friendship.

The only time Steve had seen her step out of her Psychological Judo mode was a week before Johansen was "retired" - offered a parachute rather than the option of going down with his flaming career. He had been ranting around the squad room, insulting every female within earshot and most of the males. Steve and several others were about to intervene when Kathleen entered the room, walked calmly up to Johansen, stood a few inches from his face, which involved having to look down her nose at the little man, and said a few quiet words which no one quite overheard. She then grasped his index finger, twisted it along with his arm behind his back, and said, again quietly, "Go home. Start your retirement now and you can do it without a broken finger." This time the others heard her. Johansen left, came back during the night shift and cleared out his desk, and started his retirement.

Officer Amy Hsu spoke up from behind Collins, her diminutive body hidden by his six foot five inch frame. "Excuse me Sergeant Collins, but there's someone downstairs wanting to see Lieutenant Ito, says his name is Cooper."

"Amy, come on in," Kathleen said, "if you can get by the man-mountain blocking the door."

"Didn't see you Amy," Collins smiled as he stepped back outside the door, "You must have been hidden in the haze way down there."

Amy raised her eyebrows at Kathleen to suggest, "Men!"

"I'm going across the street for a scone for breakfast. Want me to get you something," Collins said before he left.

"Hold on that a minute," Kathleen said, "I have a feeling Cooper might be bearing gifts from the oven of the Happy Frog."

"Happy Frog?" officer Hsu asked. She had recently transferred to the Newport office from Portland and was still getting the lay of the land.

"An odd sort of place down in Carson Beach," Collins answered from behind her, "Kind of a Hogwarts of the west coast."

"Hogwarts?" Hsu looked even more confused.

"Harry Potter," Collins explained.

"Harry Potter?" the thought that she might transfer back to Portland crossed her mind..

"Sergeant Collins, would you please go down and get Professor Snape a visitor's pass and escort him up. I think he is bringing Pecan Rolls all the way from Carson Beach. May not be a need for scones this morning," Kathleen used her *authority* voice with a twinkle in her eye.

"Right away, Lieutenant," Collins snapped a salute and hurried out.

"Sit down, Amy," Kathleen said, coming around her desk to sit at the small table in the corner. "I wanted to ask you how you were getting along. Don't mind Sergeant Collins. We were bantering about the Harry Potter books."

"Oh, yes," Amy said, getting the reference, "and the Happy Frog? Is that a book?"

"It's a coffee shop cafe in Carson Beach owned by a friend of mine."

At that moment, the aroma of fresh Pecan Cinnamon Rolls preceded Cooper into the office.

"Happy Lieutenant's Day to you," Cooper sang as he put the large platter down on the table.

Kathleen stood and hugged Cooper. She turned to officer Hsu and said, "Cooper, this is Officer Amy Hsu, newly assigned here from Portland. Amy, this is my good friend Jim Cooper."

"Jim Cooper," Amy said as she shook Cooper's hand, "James Cooper?"

"Yes," Cooper said, noting the curious look on Amy's face.

"Were you stationed with the Air Force in Okinawa back in the 80's?"

"Well ... yes," Cooper inclined his head to the side.

"I've been meaning to look you up," she said.

Once again Carl found himself asking, *What am I doing here?* It was early evening and The Happy Frog, since it served only breakfast and lunch, was closed and a circle of people were sitting around two large tables pulled together. A platter of fresh scones sat on one of the tables and various mugs of tea were being enjoyed. His wonderment was less worrisome than it had been. He felt a strange sense of comfort - a sort of homey feeling, but he remained puzzled by the monumental changes of the past few weeks.

Carl looked about the group: Mary and Connie, former owners of The Happy Frog; Cooper, present owner and head cook; Kathleen and Kogan, State Police Lieutenant and Family Physician respectively; and Dorothy, owner of Words and Images, bookstore and art gallery. All were relaxed and talking in "indoor" voices, no one calling attention to themselves, enjoying each other with no artifice or agenda.

These are good people, Carl thought as he sipped his tea, but there's something uncanny about the way they approach things.

Cooper was telling the group about his dinner with Amy Hsu the previous night.

"Turns out her father was a translator working with the Taiwanese diplomatic mission to Japan and was also a good friend of a pilot friend of mine when we were both stationed at Kadena Air Force Base in Okinawa. Her father and I never met but apparently Gary, my friend, had mentioned me to him. He had heard that I was in this area and asked her to give me his regards."

Cooper paused for a moment, a wistful expression passed over his face.

Mary asked, "What happened to your friend, Coop?"

Cooper stretched his neck back and forth, then poured himself a bit more tea.

"Gary flew the big KC-135 Supertankers, you know, the mid-air refueling planes. They were huge things, full of aviation fuel for refueling F-15s in flight. I was standing with some other officers just outside the legal office watching one of these big 135s take off. I recognized Gary's plane by the tail number. We just sort of idly watched as the bird lifted... then there was some sort of a shower of sparks from the belly and the wing dipped to the left and caught the tarmac."

Cooper stopped for a moment. The room was silent.

"The whole plane seemed to collapse into the wing. There were two explosions in quick succession, the first from the fuel in the wing and the second from the fuel load. The second one disintegrated the plane and broke windows in lots of buildings, including my office.

"This was more than thirty years ago and I can still remember the noise. My ears rang for a month." Cooper gave a small shrug. "It also rang a bell inside of me, sort of a wake-up bell... my first experience with the transience and unpredictability of life."

Connie broke the silence, "Did Amy's father know about the accident?"

"Yes," Cooper responded. He paused for a moment, then shook his head and said, "This was a long time ago. I think now Amy just wants to make a connection between her family and this new job she's taken on. Certainly she'll need support given the temperament of her new boss."

Kathleen sniffed a haughty reply, "She is in good hands, Mr. Cooper."

Kogan lifted his eyebrows and smiled at Cooper, "The young Miss Hsu has her work cut out for her."

"*Dozo, Ito-san,* stuff it!" Kathleen replied.

Carl silently enjoyed the banter between these intimate friends. Dorothy was sitting next to Cooper and Carl noticed that she would occasionally touch his shoulder. *Is there something there?* he wondered.

He decided to venture into the conversation. "Cooper," he asked, "What did you do in the Air Force?"

"I was with the Judge Advocate General corps. Basically I was a lawyer with a uniform."

Carl sat up, "You were actually became a lawyer then?"

"The shame comes out," Kathleen laughed.

"Um, well… yes," Cooper admitted, "but it didn't take. I'm in recovery."

"I've landed in an interesting group of people," Carl said as he shook his head. "I still feel like I'm living an unreal life." He continued, "You know, I've been here almost two months and I haven't been in touch with people in Michigan other than to let the school know I wouldn't be back and to let my parent's know that I was all right. No one really knows where I am. *I'm* not sure where I am."

Connie smiled across the table, "Carl, you're home. Didn't you know that?"

No one at the table laughed. When Connie used that tone of voice everyone assumed she was speaking more than simple reassurance. Carl felt a shiver snake up his spine. Again not frightening, but uncanny.

Carl looked at Connie, "Does every stranger in town get this kind of welcome and support?"

Connie shook her head, "Of course not, silly. This isn't home for most people."

"I see," Carl said. "Actually, I don't see."

"Do you feel at home?" Mary asked.

Carl hesitated for a moment, "Yes, I do. But I wonder why. I wonder if I should."

"Should?" Cooper asked, "Why shouldn't you?"

"I don't know. Something inside me accuses me of running away from my responsibilities."

"Responsibilities?"

Carl chuckled, "My dad mentioned that all my friends were very disappointed at my 'irresponsible' behavior."

"Ah," Cooper nodded.

Dorothy asked, "Do you have friends who are depending on you to do something particular?"

"Not really," Carl replied, "just a general sense that I should behave in a certain manner I think."

"Ah," Dorothy repeated Cooper's Rogerian response.

Kogan leaned forward, "Carl-san, don't let these people intimidate you. They are a strange group of rebels and anarchists, even my establishment wife is a closet revolutionary. They will lead you astray and soon you may find yourself being unreasonably happy and content. Be very careful."

Dorothy laughed, "Carl, the truth is that, as Connie said, we have a sense that you fit here. We could be wrong and you will have to take the time to decide for yourself. We've learned to trust Connie's intuitions over the years. But Connie's feelings aside, I think you might find something here that brought you the two thousand miles."

Carl chuckled, "Dancing feet…"

"Dancing feet?" Dorothy asked.

"A dream," Carl said, "a recurring dream. Someone dancing on a beach; a wild passionate dance, but somehow full of power and meaning."

"Whose feet are they?" Connie asked.

Carl sighed, "That's the question, isn't it?"

Chapter 9 - Paints and Puzzles

When he moved into the cottage Connie had made available for him, Carl put his painting supplies - paper, paints, brushes, and a few unfinished paintings in a corner of the small storm porch. In the weeks he had been living in Carson Beach he had not touched them; seldom even glanced their way.

This morning he stood looking at the neglected items with a glimmer of interest. The Dancing Feet appeared again in his dreams last night. On this occasion he felt the urge to join in the dance but couldn't figure out how he might do that. In the dream he was usually a disembodied observer. He had the thought upon waking that, if he could somehow learn to join in the dance, he might be closer to discovering the mystery and message of the dream. Could his painting somehow be connected with the dance?

He spread a blanket out on the little kitchen table and laid a watercolor pad on top of it. *Let's start small,* he thought, *no great ideas, just some simple brush strokes to get a feel for things.* He mixed some black sumi paint with a tiny bit of water in a small bowl, then dipped a brush in clean water. He squeezed the brush on the side of the bowl then dipped the tip in the rich black ink. He paused a moment with the brush poised over the pad, then made one long, flowing, twisting stroke with the brush, varying the pressure as he did so. It was a satisfying moment.

He continued to make brush strokes on the thick paper for a half hour or so, then felt suddenly out of energy. He looked up at the room and realized that a thought had been growing in volume for the past few minutes.

"You can't just make random marks on paper. Either paint 'something' or quit and find something worthwhile to do. You can't make a living as a painter - we both know that. Are you going to dabble for the rest of your life?"

Once activated, these thoughts led inevitably to a litany of the responsibilities he had abandoned back in Michigan, the people he had disappointed, and the wreck he was making of his life. "There's still time," the chorus intoned, "to grow up, move back to Grand Rapids and try to salvage your life."

Through the open window he heard the barking of the "old bachelors", the name given to the group of sea lions that used a pier down at the wharf area for their communal resting spot. The deep insistent tones of these strange creatures cleared his mind a bit. The ocean breeze and salty smells stirred him and he shook his head. *I've got a job to go to in an hour,* he thought, *I'll paint for another 30 minutes and then walk to work.* The voices subsided and he returned his attention to his brush and to the simple black lines filling the white paper.

Carl arrived at the *Words and Images* bookstore fifteen minutes early. He unlocked the back door and was greeted by Chi, Dorothy's Siamese cat, who lived at the bookstore, hiding away in esoteric literature nooks much of the day but emerging at night to keep the books and paintings free of rodent damage. She also waited each morning for her food and a modicum of affection. Sometimes she would curl up in the front display window as a bookstore cat is obliged to do, but her reclusive and independent streak ("*We are Siamese if you don't please...*") kept her from unwanted doting and stroking during business hours.

Carl hurried to turn off the alarm while Chi paced purring between his feet. Chi submitted to being picked up and Carl walked with her into the office and placed her by her food bowl, scooped a cup of dry food into the bowl, and refreshed her drinking water. This ended the affectionate period and Chi turned her attention to her food with a rumble of purring and chomping.

Carl turned on the lights and was walking to the front door when he noticed a new art display in the middle alcove at the north wall of the store. Dorothy must have put it up yesterday. The accent lights picked up golds and reds woven into silk hangings and highlighted the monochrome tones of black and grey of what seemed to be traditional Chinese paintings. *Interesting,* Carl thought, *I was just using sumi ink this morning for the first time in years. Now I see a new display of that art.*

Carl was standing in the alcove admiring the simple beauty of the paintings combined with the careful mounting on the silk scrolls when Dorothy walked up behind him. He jumped with a start as she touched his shoulder.

"Sorry," she said, "I didn't mean to disturb you."

"No problem," he said, returning his attention to the scrolls. "This is beautiful work."

"Yes," she said, "we were lucky to get these. They'll sell quickly."

"Where did they come from?" Carl asked, still lost in the brushwork *It looks like something from the Northern Song Dynasty,* he thought, *with the strong black lines, rocks, mountains…*

"You like them?" she answered with her own question.

"Very much," he said. "They look like the Northern School of the Song Dynasty."

"Very good," she smiled, "Who says a Fine Arts degree is wasted?"

"Well," Carl turned to her, "My parents, my school friends, my extended family, and pretty much everyone I know in Michigan."

She looked directly into his eyes. "What do *you* say?"

"It depends on when you ask me," he replied. "Right at this moment I can't think of any other degree in the world that I would value more."

He turned his attention back to the scrolls. "They are classical in style but recently painted, I think," he said, "Who is the artist?"

"Samuel Hsu," she replied, "Amy Hsu's brother. He lives in Lincoln City - a very traditional young man and a brilliant painter. He teaches part-time at Williams College just down the coast."

"It's a liberal arts college, Isn't it?" Carl asked.

"Yes. Small and expensive, but with a fine reputation for fostering the arts - writers, painters, and actors, they have a somewhat famous drama department."

Just then the door chime rang and the first customers of the morning entered - a young mother with two toddlers in tow. She and the tots headed directly for the children's corner near the rear of the store. The children's section was carefully arranged in a welcoming manner and featured some classic children's books as well as modern stories. It also had its own art display of drawings and paintings by local children. The store was truly a place of words and images.

Dorothy asked Carl to do some cataloguing of recent arrivals while she opened the front counter. As he started toward the back storage room she called to him, "Samuel Hsu is dropping by today to check the hangings. You might enjoy meeting him."

As Carl began opening the boxes of new books he murmured to himself, "Yes, yes I *would* enjoy meeting him."

"Carl drove over to Williams College this morning to talk with Professor Hsu," Cooper was saying to Connie as they worked through the familiar rituals of breakfast preparations. "I didn't realize that Amy Hsu had a brother who was a professor. She didn't even mention him when we talked. Apparently he's been in Lincoln City for a few years. Dot knows him but never mentioned him."

"You sound like you feel left 'out of the loop', Coop," Connie said as she slid a tray of Rosemary potatoes into the oven.

"Not at all," he replied quickly, "just... Yeah, I feel left out of the loop. Isn't that silly?"

She rose and patted his cheek, "Yes, dear, very silly. You can't be left out of the loop. No one can be. You might not know everything that's going on, but you're never, ever, 'out of the loop.' That's just a silly phrase the mind uses when it gets its feelers hurt."

"You mean 'feelings' hurt."

"No, 'feelers,' those long antennas that reach out looking for danger and trouble."

"Ah, 'feelers.'"

Connie dusted her hands on her Happy Frog apron and smiled, "It is nice that he's making that connection though. It's very important for him to regain his art."

"Yes," Cooper agreed, "I don't need your fey sense to see that is true. My own intuition tells me that there's something else either pushing him or pulling him as well, something he's afraid of or that he wants very badly."

"Probably something he wants," Connie nodded, "I agree. Art's part of it but not all of it."

As the breakfast crowd began to thin out around 9:30, Cooper had a moment to sit on the back patio and watch the surf in its eternal movement. *Nothing's eternal,* he thought as he watched, *even the ocean. But for my little mind it's eternal enough.*

"Lost in thought, Coop," Kathleen's voice lilted pleasantly into his awareness.

"Just lost," he replied, "and enjoying it."

"Mind if I intrude on your mystical moment with some nitty gritty?"

He looked up at her face and noticed that she had her professional countenance in place, though somewhat apologetic at the same time.

"I'm not being arrested am I?" he shifted in his chair, and motioned to the companion chair beside the small table. He stood up and said, "Have time for a coffee? I need a refill."

"Sure, Coop, that would be nice, thank you." She sat down and sighed.

Something uncomfortable about to come my way, He mused.

As they settled in with their hot mugs of comfort drink, Kathleen got down to the nitty-gritty as she promised. "Coop, I need to talk about a difficult case that's landed on my desk - well, on my department's desk."

"OK…" he hesitated.

"A scoutmaster in Newport has been accused of molesting several of the boys in his troop."

Cooper grimaced, "Shit. Really?"

"Really. I won't go into the details. Suffice it to say it is a convoluted case, filled with miserable unhappy people. Since I'm the 'expert' in forensic psychology, the whole thing has ended up in my lap."

"And you're supposed to…?" Cooper asked.

"Sort it out. Find out the truth, determine the damage, soothe the parents, protect the boys…"

"Ouch," Cooper commiserated.

"I like my job, Coop, I really do. I suffer with victims, but I enjoy the puzzle of sorting things out. I'll do it in this case and I'll probably do it well."

Her eyes brightened as she talked. "There is a great thrill in seeing pieces of evidence in a crime fall into place. It's just like a puzzle only better. An actual puzzle, you know, a game-type puzzle, is designed to be solved and, in solving it, you are just discovering the pattern deliberately created by the designer of the puzzle. That is fun - seeing if you can figure out what he or she had in mind in making the puzzle. But a crime - a crime is *not* designed to be solved, just the opposite. There is a pattern but not a deliberately designed one. It is a Meta-pattern so to speak - one that exists in the very nature of the chaos surrounding the event, despite the intentions of the criminal. A detective follows certain procedures, formulas that are helpful. But a good detective is like a theoretical physicist. She intuitively recognizes patterns no one else sees, not even the criminal."

"Uh-huh, Chaos Theory," he nodded.

"Yes! Exactly! You know many seemingly random events, like those surrounding a crime, are actually more accurately fractals."

"Oops, when I said, 'Chaos Theory," I also said everything I know about said theory. What is a fractal?"

"Well," she leaned forward, "mathematically it's complex, but the word means a small part of something that, when examined closely, looks just like the big something that it is a part of. Get it?"

"OK" *No.*

"In this case, each of the boys involved is part of the picture. Of course they're innocent victims, but each of them gives a picture of the crime through their own eyes. I somehow put all their stories together and, instead of simple moral indignation, I find out the fabric of the crime itself. That makes it much clearer for the State's Attorney to present."

"OK, I do see that," Cooper nodded.

"Now…" she said "Here's where you come it."

Oh-oh.

" One of the boys is Bobby Greenspan."

Cooper sighed, "Bobby Greenspan. Damn!" Cooper knew Bobby and his parents. They were regular customers at the Happy Frog and he often met them walking along the beach. Bobby was about twelve and his sister was around eight. "This has to be a shock for the family."

"They're handling it well, as far as I can see. But Bobby is, of course, withdrawing. There's going to be a lot of press starting tomorrow and I wanted to give you a head's up. I know you sometimes talk with the family."

"Thanks for the tip off. I often see them when I'm out for a jog on the beach. I'll stay aware."

Kathleen smiled, "Thanks, Coop. I just wanted you to know."

"Are you OK?" he asked, "I mean, really?"

She sighed, "Yeah, Coop, I am. This isn't the first trip to the dark side for me. I stay grounded in my work. Kogan, Connie, Mary, you, Dot... everyone's individual strengths feed into me, just like they do for all of us."

She stood to leave. Cooper stood with her and took her hand, "As I said, I'll stay aware. Give my best to your samurai husband."

"Hai," she bowed her head, "Sayonara, Cooper-san"

Cooper walked with her around the corner of the building and back into the kitchen. *Bobby Greenspan,* he thought, *damn!*

Chapter 10 - "Just Call Me Bob"

Cooper's night passed slowly, sleep punctuated by periods of waking and restless thoughts. He did not fight for sleep. He had learned years ago that trying to sleep was a futile effort.

On this particular night his mind was full of memories along with the usual conditioned commentary about the memories that fueled regret and melancholy. Each time he awoke his mind would be tuned to a general sadness. He would immediately get up, put on his *yakuta*, a lightweight Japanese robe, and start the burner under the tea kettle. After the water boiled he would let it sit for a few minutes, then pour it into a mug along with a strainer of blended herb tea. He wasn't sure of the herbs in the mixture. It was a blend that Dot had prepared especially for him and he didn't question her about it. He knew that, on nights like these, it was the perfect companion for his restless mind.

Sitting cross-legged on a cushion, he would sip the tea and watch his thoughts flow by. He had learned to put part of his mind into an "observer" position, from which he could let thoughts arise without either attaching to them or pushing them away. This perspective often allowed him to see the origins of his thoughts and thus be able to stop automatically assigning them meanings.

His thoughts and memories during the three or four wakeful periods of the night centered around the indictment of the Scoutmaster and the plight of Bobby Greenspan. As he watched the thoughts, he saw how they triggered memories of his own childhood. Memories, he knew, were inaccurate. Each time a memory occurred, it would be a bit different, actually a memory of a memory. As years pass, memories become modified and interpreted in numerous ways, depending on the current situation.

These memories were of his own experience with a trusted family friend and neighbor who, one afternoon when Cooper was twelve, invited him to come swimming in his backyard pool. When Cooper arrived at the neighbor's house he found that the neighbor's children were not at home.

"Where's Emily and Todd?" Cooper asked.

"They'll be along in about an hour," the man responded. "Let's go ahead and get in the pool."

Sipping his tea, Cooper watched the memory fade and blur. He had only vague images of the discomfort he felt as the man insisted they skinny dip in the pool, "After all, it's just us guys," he said. Todd and Emily had arrived before anything could progress beyond inappropriate touching. The man never made other advances to Cooper and he put the incident out of his mind as best he could. A few months later the man's family suddenly moved out of town; one day the moving van arrived and by the late afternoon the house was empty. Cooper's parents expressed surprise that they hadn't known of an impending move.

Following the memories was the usual flood of commentary, which Cooper continued to watch from a separate observation point. "How could you do that?" a voice sneered. "What a pussy you were," another said in a disgusted tone, "You should have punched him in the nose and got the hell out of there." The Observer Cooper nodded his head and said, "Yes, I could have done that, but I didn't. Do you have anything new to add?"

When such memories and commentaries are allowed to arise without clinging or resisting, they often pass quickly. Cooper yawned and put his mug beside the futon and climbed back under the covers and drifted into another period of sleep which lasted about ninety minutes before he woke to yet another feeling of melancholy.

Brewing another cup of herbal tea, Cooper let his thoughts drift to a series of memories about decisions he had made that, looking back, seemed to illustrate a deep distrust of his own masculine energies. He gravitated to girls and women as friends and depended on his "sensitive" side to cultivate relationships. Even in law school he avoided the litigation side of law, focusing on estates and property.

Again a period of dream-filled sleep culminated in another period of wakefulness and herbal tea. He watched a replay in his mind of that day in Berkeley when everything shifted. It was a mild earthquake as Bay area earthquakes go and he didn't give it much thought. As he took the bus home he heard passengers talking about a small section of I-80 that had collapsed, crushing some cars beneath the rubble. "How sad," he thought.

The tea soothed his chest as he sat quietly and let the surrealistic images of the rest of that terrible day unfold. He couldn't remember the last words he spoke to Paulette that day. He couldn't remember identifying the body that evening at the Oakland hospital.

When he woke for the final time about 5:00 a.m. he took a shower and dressed for a morning's work. He was just about to head out the door when his cell phone buzzed. Very few people had this number and wondered who would call this early. He flipped open the relatively ancient phone and answered, "This is Cooper."

"Hi, Coop," came Connie's cheerful voice, "are you going to take a run on the beach this morning?"

Why would she ask that? He wondered.

"I wasn't planning on it," he said, "I was just heading for the Frog to set up for breakfast."

"I'll set up and get the breakfast started," she chortled, "You should take a run. I would be good for you."

What on earth…?

"Why should I take a run?" he prodded.

"You should take a run," she said.

OK.

"OK, Connie, if you say I should take a run, I'll take a run - but just a short one. I'm tired, didn't sleep well last night."

"This will help," she replied with confidence.

He pulled on his sweat clothes and laced up his old New Balance shoes. Cotton gloves and an old fisherman's cap completed his running ensemble and he went out into the dark early morning fog. The phosphorescence of the surf and the dim town lights supplied plenty of illumination for running on the smooth firm wet sand.

As he warmed up into an easy jog, he blessed Connie for her fey nature. *She somehow knew I needed to stretch my legs and blow off some of the crappy voices from last night.*

He continued for about a mile, getting just as far as the group of large boulders that marked a curve where the beach turned back toward the small harbor entrance. He was about to turn around when he saw a figure sitting on one of the rocks, hunched over with his arms about his knees.

Shouldn't disturb him, Cooper thought, but then waited a moment, rehearsing Connie's words. He walked quietly toward the figure and saw that it was a young boy. The boy heard Cooper and turned his face toward him

Oh! Cooper understood... *Bobby Greenspan!*

"Good morning, Bob. I'm sorry, didn't mean to startle you," Cooper said quietly, "I was just out for an early run.

"'Morning Mr. Cooper," Bobby said, "That's O.K., I was just watching the ocean some before I headed back home."

"Yeah," Cooper said, "I like to start my day looking at the ocean. It's restful."

"Sometimes," Bobby replied, "Sometimes it's not."

"What's it like now?" Cooper asked.

Bobby shrugged his shoulders.

"Well," Cooper said, "this is the turnaround point of my run. I'm going to head back. See you later, Bob." He turned to head north up the beach.

"Mr. Cooper," Bobby said quietly.

"Hmm," Cooper turned and looked at him.

"Why'd you call me Bob?"

"Your name, isn't it?"

"Yeah, but everybody, I mean everybody, calls me Bobby. Nobody calls me Bob." He began the sentence with some force but by the time he got to, "Bob," his voice cracked and he turned his head away. "Doesn't matter," he muttered, "never mind."

Cooper stayed at a distance, not wanting to crowd or impose on the boy. "Seems to me that after what happened to you that Bob is a better name. It's a stronger name, more of a man's name."

Bobby turned a fierce look toward Cooper and cried out, "What d'you mean, what happened to me?"

Cooper said in an even tone, looking directly into the boy's eyes which were flashing with anger, "I mean the incident with your scoutmaster. People are talking about it," he paused, "Aren't they?"

"Shit!" Bobby hollered out over the waves, "shit, shit, shit!" Then he began to cry. "Of course everyone's talking about it," he said through his tears. "I was m-m-molested."

"That's an interesting word, 'molested,'" Cooper said, "what's it mean?"

"He touched me down there!" Bobby shouted with a sob, "what do you think it means? What do you *think* happened?"

Cooper replied, "I really don't care what people think it means," He leveled his words with a force that caused Bobby to flinch. "What I do care about is you." Cooper sat down on the sand in a cross-legged position, keeping his distance. "Same thing happened to me once, a long time ago," he said.

"It did?"

"Yes, but the details are none of your business, just like the details of what happened with you are none of my business - none of anyone else's business either."

Bobby sat silent for a few moments, frowning at the relentless waves. Then, keeping his face turned to sea, he said in a small voice, "You know, what really makes me ashamed is not what he did. That was just sort of strange and uncomfortable. He didn't hurt me. I didn't really know why he wanted to touch me. I didn't want him to, but I didn't feel terrified either - just uncomfortable. What make me ashamed is that I was cold and scared and asked to sleep in the Scoutmaster's tent."

"You were cold and scared. It seems perfectly reasonable to me to ask for help."

"It does?" Bobby turned toward Cooper.

"Of course. It's natural to assume that your Scoutmaster can be trusted to help. It's not your fault that you asked a person who couldn't be trusted. You did nothing to be ashamed of. Nothing," he paused, then added, "But you still feel pretty ashamed, don't you?"

"Yeah." Bobby turned back to the ocean.

"Well, that's why I called you Bob instead of Bobby. You're twelve years old now. You've had something happen that makes the world feel unsafe. You feel unsure of yourself. You don't know exactly what to do or how to feel. It's important to have something to remind yourself that you're OK. A strong name helps. It did for me when I switched from Jimmy to Cooper."

"Your name was Jimmy?"

"Well, James, or Jim, but Jimmy was what everyone called me and it felt like a little kids name to me. There came a time I wanted something sort of stronger. I tried to get them to call me Jim but people kept forgetting. Then one day the track coach from the High School called me by my last name, Cooper, and I really liked that. So from then on it was, 'Cooper' to my friends." He waited a moment, then asked, "Is it all right for me to call you Bob?"

The boy shrugged his shoulders, "Sure. It's better than 'Greenspan,' Greenspan isn't real good for a first name. Yeah, Bob is good. You'll be the only one who calls me that."

"Well," Cooper said, "things have a way of getting around. What if more people start to call you Bob?"

He shrugged again, "Guess that'd be OK."

Cooper hesitated, wondering if he should leave Bob alone with the morning ocean. He decided to risk staying just a bit longer.

"Do you mind if I come and sit on the rocks for a bit? I'd like to watch the waves for a while before I jog back."

Bob looked a bit wary, but also lonely and wanting the company, "I guess so," he said, then turned and looked out at the water.

Cooper took a seat on a low rock at a distance from Bob and turned his face to the ocean so he would not intrude into the boy's space more than he already had. He worried that he might be pushing the situation a bit, but then settled his breathing into a rhythm and let his mind empty out into the water; cleanse itself of any agenda for helping, fixing, or intruding, but simply cultivate a willingness to remain present.

They sat as the morning slowly made its way to the beach and the sand began to take on a light golden-brown hue. Cooper kept his mind free, letting thoughts of what he should say and what he should do arise and drift away. Trying to plan words in the midst of emotional situations simply narrowed one's focus and excluded possibilities.

Cooper noted that Bob sat perfectly still. *Unusual*, he thought, *for a boy his age. I certainly wasn't able to sit still back then.*

Bob startled as if waking from a dream. "What time is it?" he asked, "I should get home."

Cooper said, "I really don't know. I don't carry a watch. It's probably between six-thirty and seven."

"I told mom I'd be home around eight for breakfast. I guess I'd better be going."

"The Happy Frog is on the way from here to your home, I think. You have your bicycle, I assume. I'll race you there."

Bob smiled, liking the challenge.

"What'll you bet I can get there before you do?"

"I'll bet you a cup of hot chocolate at the Frog," Cooper replied, getting to his feet.

"Chocolate it is, " Bob whooped, then sprang up from the rock, jumped down to the sand, and dashed toward the path that led around the edge of the rocks and up through the slope to the parking lot.

Cooper smiled as he let his legs relax into a long stride. He was a natural runner, enjoying both track and cross-country in high school, the university, and the Air Force. Some of his continued motivation was for health reasons, but he actually kept running over the years because he loved it. He was addicted to the feeling that suddenly swept through his body after ten of fifteen minutes of gentle jogging. It was as if every muscle took its place as part of a highly efficient machine. His thoughts would fade, replaced by the rhythm of his footfalls and his breathing. "The Runner's High," they called it. Now in his fifties, Cooper could still capture some of the feeling of being a "good animal" - comfortable in his body, able to move swiftly and with grace.

He ran the mile and a half back to the Happy Frog in ten or eleven minutes. He stopped on the beach just below the building and waited a bit before climbing the stairs to the street level. As he got to the corner of Cliff Street, he saw Bob skid his bicycle to a stop outside the cafe. The boy stood proudly by the bike with his arms crossed over his chest. "What took you so long?" he called to Cooper.

Cooper jogged up to where Bob was standing in triumph and bent over, his hands on his knees. "Boy," he said, "you must fly on that thing. Well, come on in for that chocolate. We have plenty of time before eight o'clock."

Cooper refrained from putting his hand on Bob's shoulder. *It'll be a while before he really trusts masculine affection again,* he thought. "Let's go in and I'll make it myself."

"Mr. Cooper?" Bob said as they walked up the path through the garden to the front door."

"Yes?"

"When we're inside, would you introduce me as, 'Bob?' I'd like people to start getting used to it."

"Bob it is," Cooper nodded his head.

Bob smiled and said in a low, movie star voice, "Bob - just call me Bob."

Chapter 11 - Home

Carl sat at the small table carefully grinding the ink stick in small circles creating a smooth thick black ink in the stone grinding basin. As he worked the stick he felt a flow of gratitude for his new relationship with Samuel Hsu. Sam, as he preferred to be addressed, had turned out to be far more approachable and less intimidating than Carl had imagined. He was a skilled artist but also a dedicated teacher, feeling satisfaction and joy in his teaching position at Williams University. Whether the student was a bored nineteen-year-old in his *Introduction to Asian Art* class or an advanced student in the graduate Arts program, Sam loved giving whatever guidance and instruction he could about a subject that had been his life since his pre-teen years.

At the time of their first meeting in Sam's studio space at Williams University, provided for him by the University as their "Artist in Residence," Carl was immediately comfortable in the presence of Sam's gracious and welcoming manner. The studio was small but open and well lit through large south-facing windows that looked onto a garden grove of bamboo and evergreen trees. Sam shook hands and immediately asked Carl if he would care for some tea. He gestured to a small corner table with two chairs, partially hidden by an ornate folding screen.

While waiting for the Lost Forest Tea to steep, Sam took the initiative to give Carl comfort and "face" - the subtle art of honoring the dignity and uniqueness of an individual in a potentially difficult situation.

"Dorothy tells me that you have taken a brave journey to be here," he said to Carl, "She says there must be something guiding you to step into the unknown so boldly."

Carl lowered his head and smiled, "It seems more like insanity to me at times. I left my life behind and feel drifting and lost," he paused as Sam narrowed his eyes in a quizzical manner, "but I must admit that I also feel oddly at home here, despite all the voices screaming in my head."

"Yes," Sam nodded, "the voices screaming in our head, they are certainly a challenge." He sipped his tea and smiled at Carl, then asked, "Dorothy says that you are an artist. Do the voices bother you when you practice your art?"

Carl demurred and started to say, "I don't know if I'd be called an artist..."

Sam interrupted him at that point, forcefully, yet still politely, "Excuse me, but the voice that is saying those words is, in fact, one of those voices of which we are speaking, is it not?"

Carl was silent for a moment, not offended, but reminded of the awarenesses that were emerging in the past weeks. "Yes, they are," he said, "I *am* an artist. I have much to learn about my art, but I have been an artist for quite a few years, since high school, actually."

"Yes," Sam smiled, "we so easily adopt the word to mean someone whose work others think is valuable enough to purchase. And so often the 'others' who make these decisions are far from competent judges of another's work. Like the voices of which we were speaking, yes? Are the voices you hear competent to judge? Do they have your permission to evaluate your work? Who gave it to them?"

Carl nodded his head in agreement but qualified his nod with, "Yet, sometimes, *I* evaluate my own work and find it lacking, even poor, awful..."

Sam shook his head, "No, *you* do not evaluate your work. *They* do. It is only the voices in your head who would use words like 'lacking, poor,' or 'awful.' You *notice* your work. It expresses what you wanted to express or it does not. If it does not, you find out exactly how it does not and you do the work again. Only art critics *evaluate* art. They do not *create* art."

Carl laughed. How comfortable it felt to hear a formal artist speak such unconventional, by commercial art world standards, words out loud. Sam smiled and leaned back in his chair. "Shall I show you my studio and some of the work I do? You will not evaluate it, of course, but I would be pleased if you noticed my humble attempts to express the Tao that cannot be expressed."

They spent the next hour before Sam needed to prepare for a graduate seminar, visiting and noticing. Carl enjoyed the free, yet masterful, brush strokes of Sam's sumi paintings. He was also captivated by the wood blocks that Sam was working with; taking his own paintings, carving them in relief on cherry wood blocks, then using the blocks to print copies; an intricate and painstaking process that produced exquisite prints. Carl had seen the process demonstrated back in the art department at Michigan State. A student had asked the artist, "why such a difficult process when a high-quality printer can do just as well so much faster?" Carl remembered the silent shaking of the head as the artist said, "by all means, *you* should use a computer printer. It will keep you from cutting yourself with a chisel."

They had agreed to meet once a week for lunch on campus, just to enjoy conversation. Carl said he wanted to begin working with Sumi ink paintings and asked Sam if he had suggestions. Sam immediately invited Carl to attend his graduate seminar that met each Tuesday morning to discuss that very thing - an informal sharing seminar that Sam assured Carl would be very supportive.

"Don't go to the expense of enrolling at the University," he said, "I'll introduce you as a friend from far away Michigan and you can just listen and notice."

"You're sure that would be OK?" Carl asked.

"Of course," Sam laughed, "It is my class to teach as I wish."

Carl hummed softly as he continued to grind the ink stick until he had the fluid at the consistency he wanted. He laid the stick on a holder and took a brush from the hanging stand and dipped in in water, letting it get well soaked. Then he carefully squeezed the water out between his thumb and forefinger, leaving the brush semi-dry and ready to accept the ink. He dipped the brush tip in the ink and transferred a bit to a palette where he added a drop of water. This gave him the grey ink which he rolled the brush in until it was saturated. Then he squeezed the brush against the side of the palette, draining the excess moisture. Finally, he dipped the tip back in the black ink and held the brush over the rice paper sheet resting on a flannel pad. He was just about to make the first smooth stroke of a bamboo stem when the phone rang. Only a few people had the number of the shack so he felt obliged to answer. Not wanting to hurry his work, he laid the brush against a holder and got up and walked over to the wall phone.

"Hello, this is Carl," he said.

"Carl, honey? Hi. We got your number from your friend at the cafe or whatever it is. It's Mom, honey? Dad and I are in town for a little visit and conversation. We really want to see you, you know. We love you and want to see if we can help. Carl?.... Honey?...Are you there?"

"Yes, Mom, I'm here."

Carl sat comfortably with Cooper and Dorothy along with Kogan, and Kathleen Ito, on the deck of the Pelican restaurant and looked out at the vibrant orange, red, yellow, and violet colors of the clouds as they reflected various spectra of the setting sun. The remains of their dinner of fresh Dungeness Crab had been cleared away and Carl had been introduced to the magic of single malt Scotch for the first time.

"I'm not much of a drinker," Carl had protested, "the Ale at dinner is enough for me."

Kathleen put her hand on his shoulder and gazed into his eyes. "The Ale was not nearly enough," she said. "Cooper-san, would you go in to the bar and return with a bottle of single malt Scotch. It's all on Kogan's credit card and he can well afford it. This young man is still a bit in shock."

Carl sighed and nodded his head. "Bulldozed is the word," he said, "run over by a large truck."

The two-day visit by Carl's parents had, to say the least, not gone well. Other than being mildly impressed by the serendipitous appearance of a pod of Grey Whales whose spouts and flukes caught their eye, Milt and Cora de Wilde had focused their attentions on rescuing their son from the disastrous results of his aberrant behavior. This impromptu dinner at one of the coast's best brew pubs was, of course, Connie's idea though she and Mary were on a week-end getaway to Portland for some pampering at a luxury hotel.

"It was really that bad?" Dot asked.

"They called it an 'intervention,'" Carl said, "They were here to take me back to Grand Rapids. They had even bought a one-way ticket for me. They brought a letter from my ex-fiancee 'forgiving' me and asking me to come home. They cried. They pleaded with me. They ordered me. They shamed me. They weren't about to take no for an answer."

Cooper smiled and leaned back in his chair, putting his feet on the railing of the deck. "Yet, here you are."

Carl laughed, "Yes, here I am." He took another sip of the amber liquid which had surprised him with its smooth warmth. He held the glass up to his friends, "Here's to being here."

"So," Kathleen said, "you find The Glenlivet to your liking?"

"It's not at all like other alcoholic drinks I've tried. My experience has been mostly feeling like I was drinking gasoline. This actually has a taste, a satisfying taste." He added, "not to mention a bit of a kick." He took another sip, more of a gulp than a sip, and shuddered at the sensation.

Dot asked, "Tell us, Carl, how come you're not back in Michigan right now? With a full-court press like you experienced I'm amazed that you withstood the pressure. Were you tempted to go back?"

"Tempted isn't the word. I was feeling immense pressure to return and, after the first day I wasn't sure I could stand up to it. That night I couldn't sleep. I thought I might as well pack up my stuff and get ready to drive back. I knew I wouldn't use their goddamned airplane ticket, but I was pretty much resigned to taking the long trip home."

"Home?" Cooper asked.

"That was the key," Carl exclaimed. "Right there! I was pacing around the shack about two or three in the morning, when I realized that all the words about 'home' that my parents had been using no longer applied. Bless Connie's heart. The little shack she rented me isn't much. My parents could hardly deign to walk into it. My mother was appalled at the idea of my living, as she said, 'in poverty and squalor.' But, in those early morning hours, thinking about packing up, I realized that that wonderful little shack was my home.

"My painting supplies were spread around the room. A scroll I had just finished was hanging on the wall and my parent's wouldn't even look at it. It's a nice scroll; not at all professional, but a good start at art that I truly enjoy. I went back to bed with a sense of being at home and actually got a few hours of sleep."

Dot furrowed her eyebrows, "They didn't like that lovely scroll, the one you showed me at the bookstore?"

"Thought it was 'Eastern.' Mother wondered why I didn't paint some nice pictures of Biblical scenes."

"Oops!" Kathleen said, "that might have been a mistake."

"Big time," Carl laughed, "one among many things that helped me understand some of what I've been going through."

"Which is?" Cooper asked.

Carl smiled, "It sounds silly, but I would call it, 'growing up.' I've spent twenty-five years being a nice Christian boy. I've been ashamed of being an artist. I've assumed I needed a better-paying profession. I've related to women by trying to be sensitive and caring. As I heard my parents rehearse all those things over and over, I realized that I'm not that person any more."

"Who are you?" Ito asked with a serious tone.

"I don't know," Carl replied, "but I know that I'm not that."

"Good answer," Ito nodded his head.

The vivid sunset colors had faded and the clouds on the horizon were now a dark purple. The breeze had died but the evening was chilly. A waitress came on to the patio and lit a butane heater which immediately brought a circle of warmth to the group. As Cooper stood and stretched, Carl felt a sudden disappointment that the evening might be drawing to a close. He was delighted when Cooper picked up the Glenlivet bottle and refreshed each glass.

Carl leaned back and sipped from his glass. "I'm not that nice Christian boy anymore," he repeated.

Kathleen raised her glass to him, "No longer a boy, that's for sure. No longer Christian - perhaps. But without question still very nice."

Carl felt the warmth of Kathleen's toast and the sudden awareness of, for want of a better word, *love* for the people around him. *Maybe it's just the heat from the butane stove,* he thought. Something was beginning to click into place. He had a memory of that first day, more than three months ago, when he stood beside his pickup, confused, exhausted, and lost. He saw again the "Welcome Traveler" sign outside the front garden of The Happy Frog. He remembered the disconcerting welcome the Connie extended him as he walked in the door.

"Is Connie really psychic?" he suddenly asked out loud.

Cooper laughed. Kathleen smiled, "My dear sister-in law," she said, "does not fit any label we have tried to give her over the years. The moment you dismiss her as an airy-fairy new ager, she does something that shows a deep store of true wisdom."

Cooper added, "She won't use the word, 'psychic.' She simply 'knows things.' How she knows what she knows, I have no idea. But, I think you've seen, Carl, that when she uses a certain tone of voice, it would be wise to take her seriously."

"I do," Carl said. "When I first walked in the door of The Happy Frog, among the many things she said to me was, 'You're looking for a home, aren't you, dear?'"

Dot laughed, "Yes, that's Connie."

Carl continued, "Then she said, 'Carson Beach is a good place to look.'" He swirled the small glass of Scotch and took a sip. "She was right."

Cooper said, "It's a good place to look for a home?"

Carl replied, "It's a good place to *find* a home." He raised his glass and said with a catch in his voice, "Here's to being home."

"To being home," everyone agreed.

Chapter 12 - Unpredictable

Dot Waters sat in a small chair in the corner of her kitchen, sipping her hot chocolate and reading from an old hardback edition of Ed Abby's *Desert Solitaire* that she had found in the used section of the store. Her short bangs touched her forehead and she absently brushed them with her fingers as she looked up at Cooper. She took a moment to return her mind from the natural beauty of Arches National Monument to the here and now of her kitchen. She raised her eyebrows at Cooper who was engrossed in stirring a "catch-all" vegetable soup and adjusting the gas flame to just the right level, held up the book and sighed, "This man writes beautifully and with incredible passion." Then she skewed her mouth into a wry grimace, "Of course he is a misogynist curmudgeonly asshole."

Cooper's keen sense of self-preservation warned him to remain silent.

"Well," she said, putting a clear question mark in her voice.

He took a breath and smiled. There was no way he was going to walk deliberately into the tall grass of this conversation, so he turned his attention back to the soup, "Do you have any sage in your spice collection?"

She grinned in triumph, closed the book, got up and brought it along with her chocolate over to the stove and stood next to him. "You're not going to defend a fellow member of your sex? Is there no gender loyalty?"

Oh well, he thought, *I might as well wade in.* "I wouldn't think of defending Ed," he said. "He would scoff at my defense and leap to agree with your assessment. He would have called your words insightful and accurate. He would have then had his agent quote you on the jacket of his next book, especially the, '...writes beautifully...' part."

"People who are whole are so interesting," she said as she laid her hand on the somewhat battered book cover. "Abbey was a whole person. He lived all parts of his being. That's what makes this book so powerful." She walked over to the small wood table that sat by the window that opened to her kitchen garden.

"See," Cooper smiled, "I don't have to defend him. If I wait for a bit you'll defend him yourself."

She sipped her chocolate and looked out the window into her garden. The window was open and the evening air of carried the faint distant sound of the surf and the splashing of the fountain. "I love paradox in people." She looked back at Cooper, "That's why I like you."

"I'm a paradox?" He returned her gaze, captivated by the directness and clarity in her eyes and in the husky timbre of her voice.

"Very much a paradox," she smiled and looked into her mug. She took another sip and let her tongue swirl for a moment in the chocolaty foam, then returned it to her slightly open mouth and savored the sweet taste. "You are very much like Ed Abbey."

"I'm a misogynist asshole?"

"No, of course not," she cocked her head to one side and stared at him. "You have the same unpredictable passion. It's not necessarily a passion for causes, but for the ordinary beauty of life, which by its very nature is unpredictable. If a person loves life, as you do, he is of necessity unpredictable and passionate. I'm the same way. What I'm thinking right now, however," she continued as she leaned back and took a long drink of her chocolate, "might be very predictable."

"I wouldn't dare to guess," he said.

"I'm thinking of kissing and tasting every inch of your body."

Cooper took a deep breath. "You know," he said, "that not at all what I would have predicted."

"How wonderful. I'd hate to be predictable," she said as she stood and walked over to him. She took his hand and led him to her bedroom where she commenced her unpredictable explorations. Cooper was surprised, delighted, and bemused. She had switched from literary critic to wanton woman in the space of a few moments and he hadn't fully caught up with either her actions or his own reactions. She made little murmuring sounds and seemed in no hurry, savoring what she was doing and at the same time doing it as if it were a very ordinary and natural thing to do. The ordinary beauty of life, by nature unpredictable. Though Cooper and Dorothy had been friends ever since his arrival in Carson Beach, only in the past year had their friendship become intimate. Both valued their privacy, so the intimacy had been somewhat tentative, almost shy, until now. It had actually been many years since Cooper had experienced the natural sensuality of a woman who was unburdened by conditioned roles, stories, and inhibitions.

His initiation to sexual pleasure had occurred in Japan. He was 19 years old and had just arrived in Edo for a month of travel and language study before entering Berkeley in the fall. Though "Westernization" had begun in Japanese culture, a simple acceptance and deep appreciation of sexuality still remained in many people. It was a sensuality devoid of the double bind of pleasure/shame that had been Cooper's conditioning as a teenager in America.

That day with Aki remained in his memory as the transformative moment in his sensual life, a moment that healed much of his learned shame and did as much to set him on his spiritual journey as any religious ritual might have done. It was a treasure of simple and pure pleasure that got buried for many years by the trinkets he offered himself when he returned to America.

He remembered the softness of her hand as she took his and led him to the futon that was arranged where sunlight filtered through shoji screens to illuminate it. He remembered her breasts, the first he had seen outside of Playboy Magazine and awkward gropings in the back seat of his parent's Buick. Everything about that afternoon with Aki was soft in his mind. His own hardness was a yang counterpoint to the yin of her body. Merged with each other, the Yin and Yang ceased being two things and became the One Thing - The completed circle. He had since then experienced moments, sexual and otherwise, that brought a heightened sense of pleasure and awareness that equalled that moment, but never any that had surpassed it.

He was deeply grateful for that early healing introduction to sexuality and sensuality. For all the pain and unconscious dysfunction of the years to follow, he never lost the awareness that sight, sound, touch, taste, and smell were his primary fields of study. His maiden aunts (whose disapproving tight-lipped faces still lived deep in his psyche) would label his experiences with Aki as, "intemperate and self-indulgent." They were not that. They were sensitive and mindful touches of the truth that life is both beautiful and transient, and that appreciation of the senses is the only intelligent response to this beauty and this transience. His experience was by no means intemperate. It was tempered by a natural discipline, a deep mindful awareness that is essential for the true appreciation of sensuality.

Aki's words so long ago were still clear in his mind: "Cooper-san, we could engage in pillowing all night, bringing each other the greatest of pleasures, and still be moderate in our loving. In fact, only moderation would allow us such a night. Gently savoring, rising and falling, feeling each little twinge of sensation as a thing itself to be tasted and appreciated - this is what makes the difference between a lover and an animal."

When Dorothy had succeeded in removing his clothes, she quickly slipped out of hers. Cooper felt nineteen years old again. There was no shyness or hesitation between them and the night passed with pleasure, passion, laughter, and even some hours of deep restful sleep. The morning brought a new tenderness to their relationship and as Dorothy brewed an early pot of coffee before Cooper had to open the Happy Frog, and as Cooper sipped his coffee a sort of shyness returned, not an uncomfortable feeling but something new to their friendship, something unpredictable.

Chapter 13 - Cioppino

The weather had shifted and the first of the winter storms was building along the coast. The waves were beginning to wear their white caps with abandon. Rain would soon start to tip from vertical to horizontal and sea foam would cover the windows facing the cliff like the fire retardant sprayed on airport runways before a wheels-up landing.

Cooper didn't mind the winter storms, usually. This evening, however, he was in a restless mood that the moaning wind and rattling window frames magnified. He found himself wandering around the cottage with the vague feeling that something needed doing but whatever it was didn't reveal itself. Andy used to say that restlessness was a classic distractive technique we use to keep ourselves skipping along the surface of life. Some event invites us to probe with greater depth into some aspect of our life and our conditioned mind starts to back away; to distract us and keep us from facing uncomfortable feelings. "Restlessness" is often the name we give to the resulting tension.

What am I backing away from? thought Cooper.

Well, said a sarcasm-laden voice in his mind, *Ya think it might be Dorothy Waters?*

Enough of this, he thought. *If I'm going to distract myself, I may as well do it right!*

He dressed, put on his raincoat and rain pants and headed out into the darkness. A treat was in order, something special and out of the ordinary. He turned right on Cliff Street and headed through the rain toward the Whaler Hotel.

The Whaler was an historic building, recently renovated by Ken Richie and Paul Nestor, partners who saw hotel hospitality as an art rather than a business. Cooper felt a sense of secret delight at entering the posh lobby.

Kenny was sitting at the concierge's desk and looked up from the book he was reading. "Coop! Welcome to the rich folks world. What brings you out in the rain?"

"I'm slumming, Kenny. Every now and then you need to be exposed to those less fortunate than you. To see how they manage to scrape together scraps of pleasure from their otherwise drab and meaningless existence. Anybody around I can unobtrusively watch and pity?"

Kenny laughed. "I think there are one or two in the bistro. Not many around in mid-week December"

"Actually," Cooper said, sitting on the edge of the counter, "I was hoping Paul was in the kitchen this evening. I'd love to sit with him and a bowl of his cioppino along with fresh sourdough bread. I want a treat. It's been a dreary day but I'm now in the mood for pleasure."

"You're in luck," Kenny said, "he's holding down the kitchen duty tonight and is probably bored stiff, if you'll excuse the phrase." Kenny and Paul were lovers, life partners, and the truly interesting element in the luxurious atmosphere of The Whaler. "I'll call him and tell him you're here." Kenny picked up the phone and pushed a button. "Darling," he gushed in his best gay voice, "you'll never guess who's coming for dinner." He paused and winked at Cooper. "It's Mister Cooper of the Satisfied Toad come a-slumming." He laughed at whatever Paul's response was. Cooper could only imagine. Kenny hung up the phone and pointed down the hall. "The matridi will show you to a table you may find satisfactory. Enjoy."

"What are you reading?" Cooper asked him as he slid down from his perch on the counter.

"P.D. James." he said, *"The Lighthouse.* Cunningly wicked and engrossing. Of course," he went on, "I adore the old girl and was devastated when she passed last year. A slight twist in my makeup and I could have been off to England to make her last years a delight."

"Old girl?" Cooper feigned shock, "It's Baroness James I believe. Watch the way you talk about your betters."

"Yes," Kenny raised his eyebrows, "and wouldn't I have been an imposing Baron James-Richie?"

"Hmm," Cooper gave a mocking grin.

Kenny laughed, "Yes, yes. We could have been the Baroness and Baroness James-Richie. Off with you now. Go bother Paul."

Cooper bowed a formal court bow to him and walked down the hall to Kenny's falsetto impression of P.D. James.

The restaurant had no need of a Matridi on a slow winter evening. Paul himself greeted Cooper at the entrance, bowed, and asked in the most formal of tones if he would please follow him, that his table was ready for him. Paul was the perfect archetype of a chef. He was large in all directions, had a booming voice, an infectious laugh, and could affect a haughty manner that would intimidate a French food critic. Cooper followed his imposing figure replete with white apron and tall chef's toque through the restaurant to the stares of a few curious patrons. They reached the door to the kitchen which Paul pushed open and said, "Right through here sir."

Cooper laughed and walked through into the kitchen. Paul followed him and when the door swung shut grabbed Cooper in a bear hug that almost asphyxiated him. He stood back and clapped Cooper on the shoulders. "Coop, you have rescued me from an evening of despair and misery. You have walked into my kitchen and raised my hopes from the cellar, if not to the roof, at least to the main floor. It's been a day, my friend."

"Lots of that going around," Cooper said, "I'm here to be rescued by you, or at least by your Cioppino."

"You are most fortunate," he smiled, "I seem to have made that very stew against the possibility that someone of breeding and culture might find their way through the rain in search of the pleasures of taste. I also," he smiled, "have at my disposal a bottle of Winter's Hill 2008 Syrah - a modest wine but one I have been meaning to enjoy with the Cioppino when I got the chance." As he said this he walked over to a small table nestled in a nook against the wall. "Sit, sit, my friend."

Paul opened a small cooler and took out a bottle of wine, uncorked it, and set the bottle on the table. "I hope it meets with your satisfaction, sir," he said.

"Sit down, Paul," Cooper said, "I'm in need of company without fuss."

He looked at Cooper for a moment and said, "Yes. I'll just check on the dining room and get a loaf of sourdough." He hurried off and returned in under a minute with a fresh loaf of bread on a cutting board, a saucer of olive oil sprinkled with grated parmesan cheese, a bread knife, and two wine glasses. The aroma from the warm bread transformed the somewhat sterile industrial kitchen into a place of intimate comfort and friendship. He poured the wine and sat down. Cooper ignored the knife and almost burned his hands pulling off the end of the crusty bread. He dipped the bread in the oil and cheese and chewed with some relief. He was hungry and hadn't really known it until that moment.

Paul smiled and took a sip of the wine. He had put aside the chef persona and sat silently. Cooper enjoyed another bit of bread and some wine before breaking the silence. "I've been restless this evening. I can't seem to settle down. The storm is bothering me, and you know that storms are usually something I relish. Maybe I'm getting old."

"Getting old?" Paul echoed.

Cooper looked at him for a moment. "Paul, I hope that all therapists have non-directive responses as good as yours are."

Paul laughed and bounced out of his chair. "Cioppino! We need lots of tasty fishy stew." He hurried over to a large cook pot and removed the lid. Using a ladle he filled a huge bowl with mounds of clams, mussels, shrimp, scallops, and whitefish along with tomato chunks and who knows what else in a broth whose aroma suddenly filled the room. Bringing two smaller bowls, napkins, and spoons with him he brought the stew and sat it between them on the table.

Without a word he filled his bowl and then Cooper's. Cooper was aware of a great sense of contentment as a good friend set about sharing food and conversation with him. Confucius knew that food, drink, and friendly conversation were the at the center of a good life. Cooper knew it too.

Cooper and Paul talked of things great and small. Paul was worried about a dip in reservations from parents of university students who were the mainstay of the hotel / restaurant. Locals would occasionally treat themselves to the cuisine of Chez Paul, but IHOP, and Round Table were the routine food of choice. The Happy Frog fit comfortably in the middle and was, well, different. But Paul and Kenny were doing well. Kenny's art sold well in San Francisco and Portland and Paul had steady royalties from Cozy Mysteries he wrote under the pseudonym, "Francis DeVille." Their house in Otter Rock, about five miles north of Newport, was a truly beautiful home.

Cooper talked of his confusion about his relationship with Dorothy. They had been friends and occasional lovers ever since Cooper arrived in Carson Beach, but remained quite independent, enjoying the relationship but from a comfortable distance. There was something about the intensity of last nights love-making that both delighted and disturbed Cooper.

"I would have said I was unconventional in my view of relationships," Cooper confided, "but some part of me is nervous about an increased sense of intimacy with Dot. She's not suggesting a marriage or live-in or anything like that but..."

"But," Paul said, "you're getting closer than is comfortable for someone inside of you."

Cooper thought for a moment, savored a spoonful of cioppino, dipped a chunk of bread in the oil and chewed it quietly, then said, "I suppose so. I would have said that I am comfortable with the transience of life, the inevitability of loss, that I was not 'attached' to things or people. But, of course, I am attached. I love my friends and would feel their loss deeply..."

"But that's not quite it," Paul said quietly, "this is different somehow, isn't it?" He tipped a splash of wine into his glass, then into Cooper's. "Does it have to do with Paulette's death so long ago?" he asked.

"I wouldn't have thought so," Cooper replied, "but I have been thinking of Paulette a lot recently; also lots of dreams that involve her."

Paul remained silent and sipped his wine. The kitchen was quiet for the moment and the only sound was the whir of fans.

Cooper noticed that his wine glass was empty. Paul noticed Cooper's noticing and immediately refilled the glass with the cool white Oregon wine. Cooper smiled and took a sip.

"My memories of Paulette are growing vague," he said. "It's been a long time since her death. Her presence in my dreams, though, is very vivid."

Paul laid his spoon beside his plate and leaned forward, "But it's not the 'real' Paulette in the dreams, is it?"

Cooper thought a moment. "No, of course not. It is the 'internal Paulette' I've constructed over the years. Jung would say all elements of dreams represent the Self in some aspect."

"So," Paul said, "You're dreaming of some part of your own Psyche that is appearing as Paulette.?"

"Something like that. Of course the images are built of actual memories, distorted by time. But they are just images and may be communicating something I need to see."

"You believe dreams are messages?" Paul asked.

"I don't 'believe' anything about dreams, I don't think that they have any meaning other than the meaning I assign them, Paul. They just occur. They may be random firings of mental neurons. But I experience them. Right now, these dreams of Paulette are compelling and may be helpful to me. I'm more restless than usual. It may be Dot. It may be something else."

"You're trying to figure it out?"

Cooper smiled again at his friend, "Your imitation of Carl Rogers is wonderful, client-centered non-directive therapy at its best."

Paul smiled and gave an exaggerated, "Um-hum?"

Cooper leaned back. "Seriously, I appreciate it. And, no, I'm not trying to figure it out. I'm just watching it and describing it. It's been my experience that I don't have to figure things out. Trying to do so just muddies the waters. Best to sit still, watch, and let the mud settle to the bottom."

A companionable silence ensued. Paul would occasionally get up to check on the operation of the dining room. Between them they drank the bottle of wine and, incredible as it seemed as Cooper looked back later, finished the cioppino. Paul offered to open another bottle of wine but Cooper begged off. He had made the journey from his dissatisfied mind back to his always easy to please body. He was ready to go home.

Paul had listened as a friend would and, as a friend would, told Cooper to, "Get a grip, my friend, you and the beautiful Dorothy will be together in some form or another for the rest of your lives. Get used to it!"

"Paul, my friend, you have taken a poor hungry soul and fed him with friendship and fish. What more can I ask of you?" Cooper said as he stood to leave.

"Coop," he said somberly, "I am happy to feed and entertain you. Don't be afraid of Dorothy. You and she are quite capable of sorting out whatever is happening with you. You are both exceptionally aware people. Enjoy!"

"I will. Later, my friend. Come over to the, as Kenny says, 'Satisfied Toad' some morning and have a real breakfast."

"Breakfast? I have heard tell of such a meal. What an interesting concept," he laughed.

Back at his cottage, Cooper listened to the rain that had increased along with the wind. The windows of his cottage, solid and secure, still rattled and a voice whispered in the back of his thoughts, trying to put him on edge. The voice annoyed him a bit, but unlike the wind and rain, it was a phantom, an illusion with no energy behind it other than what he chose to give it. This evening, with cioppino in his stomach, a glass of The Glenlivet at his elbow, and the oil lamp illuminating his own copy of *The Lighthouse*, he felt a confidence that himself, Dorothy, Paul, Kenny, Carl, and all the others were quite capable of their lives.

Chapter 14 - Sanctuary

Carl watched a whale spout a few hundred yards off shore and waited to see if he could see a fluke as the whale turned back down. Sure enough, there it was, a tail raised in the air as if waving good-bye as the whale continued its journey.

As he sipped his coffee and continued to gaze out the window of The Happy Frog, Carl mused at the strange twists and turns that had delivered this midwestern boy to the Pacific coast. *I'm watching a whale, for goodness sake.* His memories of the past few months, living in a small cottage/shack in Carson Beach, Oregon, working part-time in a quaint combination book store/art gallery, meeting an odd but beautiful collection of new friends, and beginning to paint once again all formed a surreal mixture in his mind. As a college student he had played with the intellectual niceties of living in the "present moment," without plans or goals - thoughts that had a strange appeal to him then but were quickly dismissed as impractical and irresponsible. *Lord,* he thought, *I'm becoming a... a bohemian, a "hippie," for god's sake.*

He smiled at Connie as she picked up his mug and took it back to the counter for a refill without asking. *Connie never asks because she usually knows the answer before the question arises.* She was certainly an interesting person, one of the 'odder' of the odd assortment in his life. She brought a full hot mug back to the table and set it down carefully. She looked over his shoulder out the window and pointed.

"Look!" she said, "a whale's going to spout very near the shore, just a hundred yards or so out."

Carl followed her pointing finger. He saw nothing. "Did I miss it?" he asked.

"No," she replied, "not yet."

He looked again. Suddenly a geyser of water erupted very near the shore and a large grey body humped up and forward, disappeared, then spouted again before turning a huge fluke high in the air and slapping the surface with a sound that could be heard through the windows of the cafe.

"Wow!" Carl exclaimed," and turned to Connie, "How did you know...?" he started to ask, but Connie was already back at the counter talking with Mary. Carl shook his head and grinned. Trying to fathom the fey nature of Connie was beyond his abilities and he was content to watch the surface of the ocean in case he got another greeting from the whales.

Mary had gathered her medical kit and other gear as she prepared to drive down the coast to the Northwest Wildlife Sanctuary where she was the Director of Veterinary Services. She came over to Carl's table and stood looking as another whale spouted a greeting. "They're active today," she said.

"I'll say," Carl replied.

Mary stood silent for a moment looking at Carl, then said, "Carl, are you working at the bookstore today?"

"No," Carl responded, "I've got the day to paint and plan."

"Plan what?"

"My life," he smiled.

"Ah," she said, "good. I'm glad it's nothing important. Come with me down to the Sanctuary and spend the day. You haven't seen my work place yet and I'd enjoy talking with you. Deal?"

Why not? he thought, "Deal." He put a five dollar bill on the table for his coffee and toast, stood, and grabbed his green all-weather jacket. It was going to be a "misty" day the weather station reported. "Misty" on the Oregon coast meant that the rain would come straight down rather than straight across as was often the case in the winter.

Mary's red hair was tied up under her Tilly hat. The wide-brimmed hat and her many-pocketed vest gave her a safari guide appearance that suited a wild animal vet. She played with the image, sometimes taking herself seriously, but most of the time enjoying the joke. Today she was in a joking mood and looking forward to having Carl as company for the day. Connie would be busy in the kitchen with Cooper.

Mary loved Connie deeply and she appreciated the eccentric circle of people who gravitated to *The Happy Frog,* but she also enjoyed the self-contained nature of her work at the Sanctuary and found a sense of peace and calm among the wilder and more primal life that thrived in the Northwest mountains and forests. She also liked Carl. For some reason her circle of family and friends had instantly welcomed this young man into its company and she wanted to get a feel for the qualities that enabled that welcoming to occur.

Carl climbed into the tall cab of Mary's F250 pickup, looking forward to a day that promised to bring yet one more new experience to his life. Most days had been like that since he arrived on the Oregon coast back in July. He still wondered what he was doing here and where his life was headed, but the wondering had ceased to be worrying. He was at home with the wild uncertainty of the ocean, the weather, and his future because he was, in some unfathomable sense, at home with himself for the first time.

They drove south down Highway 101 through Yachats, a village with a small fishing fleet and a large amount of new money invested in massive homes that dotted the steep hillsides above the highway. The view was spectacular and those from the San Francisco area who sold their homes for huge profits before the economy went south, could invest in property here and erect the mansions they always thought they wanted. The long-time residents of the village were happy to have their restaurants and boutique shops thrive and they planned to rake in as much of this inflated money as they could before the newcomers realized that the ocean, weather, and essential wildness was suitable only to a certain personality and abandoned their palaces for civilization once again.

They crossed the bridge over the Yachats river and in a couple of miles they came to a large redwood sign that proclaimed that the Northwest Wildlife Sanctuary was off to the left and was "open to the public Wednesday through Sunday 9 AM to 4 PM." Mary turned on the paved road and in half a mile came to the parking lot of the Sanctuary. It was Monday and only ten or so cars belonging to staff were parked along the tall fence that extended from both sides of the information building.

"Here we are," Mary said with a note of pride in her voice, "welcome to the wild world of animals." She touched Carl's shoulder and said, "I hope you enjoy it. It's my special world."

"I'm honored that you would bring me," he said sincerely.

She smiled and patted his shoulder. "Let's see what's happening inside."

The Northwest Wildlife Sanctuary began forty years ago as a private zoo, established by Clara Bartholomew, the wealthy widow of a timber baron. During their twenty years of marriage she had loved her husband in her own way, but he saw the still somewhat pristine forests as an exploitable resource while she saw them as a mysterious world where life unfolded, as she said, "as nature intended to be." When Thomas Bartholomew fell victim to a rip saw accident in one of his own sawmills, Clara grieved in a manner appropriate to a wealthy widow; she began spending his fortune on projects that pleased her.

In the early 1960s, the fate of America's wilderness was already sealed, though only a handful of people, characterized as "hippies" and "tree-huggers" were protesting. Clara saw the future of the forests and found it to be bleak. She set about spending her considerable wealth to insure the care of all creatures, great and small, of the Northwest forests. Her dream was to establish a Forest Sanctuary, a refuge where injured, orphaned, and otherwise at risk animals could be cared for in a natural setting. It soon became apparent that only a small percentage of these animals could return to the forest with a good chance of survival, so the Sanctuary slowly evolved into a combination rehabilitation facility and a regional animal park. In 1971, Clara turned the first shovel of dirt on the site that was today the Northwest Wildlife Sanctuary.

Forty-four years later, Carl de Wilde and Mary O'Hara walked together through the side entrance a few feet from the spot where Clara stood and tossed a shovel full of dirt on the shoes of a county supervisor whom she felt was still taking kickbacks from the timber industry.

"Before I give you a tour, I want to check on an injured raccoon that was brought in yesterday," Mary said as she guided Carl around the side of the information center and down a trail toward the infirmary. What buildings Carl could see were designed in such a way that, rather than calling attention to themselves, blended organically with the forest surroundings. Their location, color, and form made them seem "grown" rather than constructed.

"This is a beautiful place," Carl said. "It doesn't feel like an animal hospital."

"It is more like a wildlife park," Mary said, "I hate to use the word, 'zoo,' but it is a zoo in the best sense of the word; a place where people can make a somewhat natural connection with the life around them that would otherwise go unnoticed."

They came to a low building nestled in a dense stand of huge fir trees. A small wooden sign by the door identified it as the "Bartholomew Infirmary," and a sign on the door indicated, "staff only, please." Mary unlocked the door and invited Carl inside.

"Good morning Doctor O'Hara," said a tall young man stooping over a stainless steel table and stroking a somewhat befuddled raccoon that was attempting to gain purchase on the slippery table top - an impossible task given her sedated mind and splinted legs.

"Morning Mike," Mary said as she hung up her coat, hat, and umbrella by the door, "Meet my friend, Carl. Carl, this is Mike, my very favorite vet tech."

"Her only vet tech," Mike smiled as he shook Carl's hand. Mary turned her attention to the raccoon. "How's she doing, Mike?"

"The splints set solid. She's woozy but doing fine, but..." Mike hesitated.

Mary turned to him, "What?"

"Well, Suzi took a turn for the worse last night. You might want to take a look."

Mary sighed and hurried away down a corridor to the left. Mike looked at Carl and shrugged his shoulders. "Suzi?" Carl asked.

"Suzi is an older Bobcat. Lost a foot in a trap about ten years ago and has been pretty much of a pet around here since. She has a bladder infection that doesn't want to clear up... makes her pretty miserable."

Mary reappeared at the door to the corridor. "I'm afraid I'm going to be here for awhile this morning. Carl, would you mind giving yourself a walking tour? You'll have the place all to yourself. There's free coffee at the administration building. I'll meet you at the canteen there in, say, an hour?"

"No problem," Carl said, "I'll enjoy exploring and maybe sketching a bit."

"Thanks, Carl," Mary smiled, "I'll see you in an hour."

Carl sat by the Timber Wolf habitat and watched in silence while golden eyes watched in return. *What mental processes are going on in his mind?* Carl wondered. He was mesmerized by the wolf's stare, almost as if the animal was quietly seeking to establish dominance, to settle who's who in this strange pack of two so different, yet not-so-different, beings.

Carl carefully opened his sketch book, trying not to break the connection. The wolf didn't flinch. Carl opened his brush-pen and held it poised over the paper for several minutes while he took in the energy of that wild beautiful face. He knew it would be useless to make any attempt at drawing a "realistic" figure. *You could never, even in a photograph, capture what I'm seeing and feeling,* he thought.

Remembering Sam Hsu's advice; "See how few brush strokes can you use to capture the essence of the subject. Then make the strokes without thinking and without effort," he took his eyes off the wolf for a moment and made one, two, three, four, five, six... and seven brief strokes. Then he stopped and returned his attention to the wolf. Again he heard Sam's voice, "Once you have made your strokes, forget them for at least three days. Don't think about them at all. Then, when it is time, return to them and find out what they say. You will crumple and toss at least 90% of them, but a few you will keep and study to see what you did that worked."

Carl looked at his brief impression of the wolf's gaze. Immediately he began to hear a voice telling him of the futility of his efforts. He smiled and turned the page in the sketchbook to a new blank sheet. *Wait three days.* he said to himself. He turned his attention back to the golden eyes which were still regarding him with a primal intelligence. He forgot the previous sketch and held his brush poised over a clean page, waiting to draw what was there, now.

Chapter 15 - The Reluctant Reverend

The Happy Frog was always open on Christmas morning. Traditionally the morning is set aside for being at home with loved ones. For a certain number of people, The Happy Frog was that home.

Tom Morton, the pastor of the First Congregational Church in Carson Beach, was waiting at the door when Cooper opened. That a clergyman would be at the Happy Frog on Christmas morning did not surprise Cooper. Tom was what Cooper called a "reluctant Reverend." He had that haunted look in his eye, sort of like he was constantly wondering just what had happened to his life. A look that seemed to say, "Who are all these people sitting on uncomfortable benches looking up at me and why do I want to drop my pants, moon them, and run screaming into the night?"

Cooper liked Tom. He felt that somewhere in Tom's youth or childhood he learned that being nice, polite, reverent, and helpful was the key to his survival. Nice children reap rewards from authority. *They also get quite messed up,* Cooper thought. They abandon the not-so-nice, but oh-so-potent parts of their personality at an early age, usually never noticing that they are doing so. Sooner or later these abandoned personas cause enough stink down in their basement dwellings to make life very uncomfortable. Cooper felt that Tom's life was very uncomfortable, but he did like the man.

"Merry Christmas, Tom."

"If you say so, Coop," he said. "Mmm, it smells good in here. What a pleasant place to be on a dreary Christmas morning." Cooper had several thick chicken basil sausages on the grill along with onions and potatoes. Among the very few things he knew for sure was how to make a cold morning welcoming. It's done with aromas and tastes.

"I am your first Christmas customer, I assume," he said as he slid onto a stool at the counter near the grill.

"The very first," Cooper said, flipping the sausages and giving the onions a stir.

"Any special discount for being first?"

"Your pick of mugs." The Happy Frog had an eclectic collection of coffee mugs arranged on a shelf unit that sat on the counter. Not your usual mugs with advertising slogans and chipped handles, these were all hand-made by various potters in town. People had their favorites but it was first-come, first served.

"Ah," Tom smiled. He considered the collection for a moment, then picked a large blue/green cup with a bit of Kanji lettering on one side.

"Good choice," Cooper said. He filled Tom's mug and sat it in front of him, then refilled his own and sat down on the ever-present portable stool he kept around to give his feet and legs as much ease as possible. Cafe cooks know how to treat their feet.

"What are you reading lately?" Cooper asked. Tom loved to read. Cooper knew that being clergy was a scary profession but, as Tom had said, it was at least one of those jobs where you can get paid for reading as well as deduct the cost of almost any book from your income tax. After all, you have to keep informed on the politics and literature of your parish. Cooper thought reading might be all that was keeping Tom from flying apart.

Tom looked down at the book bag that was his constant companion. "Hmm," he said, rummaging around in the bag and pulling out a small yellow-covered book. "This one's called *Wide Awake*. It's about insomnia. Kind of a clever take on the whole theme."

"Having trouble sleeping?"

"Sometimes," Tom grimaced.

The sound of the door opening caused them to look up and see a man and woman enter. Cooper did not recognize them. He thought that they might be visitors here for the holidays. Their faces showed that combination of good cheer and weariness that often accompanies travelers at this time of year.

"Merry Christmas, friends," he called out. "Please sit anywhere you like. Would you like some coffee?"

They both affirmed a coffee need. They seemed pleasant people, soft-spoken. They took a table by the south windows. Cooper poured two mugs of coffee and served them. Just then he heard Connie arrive through the kitchen door. She came bustling into the room with her usual morning cheer and quickly took over the serving, working her magic on the bemused couple.

Cooper returned to the grill and picked up his spatula and the conversation with Tom.

"What keeps you awake?"

"Waiting to go to sleep. Watching and asking, 'Am I asleep yet?'"

"Yeah, though there are some activities that are best done consciously, falling asleep is certainly not one of them. It's sort of like continually checking to see if your heart's beating."

"Um-huh. I do that sometimes too."

"And?"

"So far, every time I've checked it's been beating."

"That's a relief."

Connie came over and leaned her arm across Tom's shoulder and kissed him on the temple, "Hi Rev. Tom. Coop, two scramble combos. Sorry I'm late."

The Happy Frog had a limited menu, serving only the food that Cooper and Connie enjoyed serving. The breakfast menu was usually five or six cooked-to-order choices plus a small assortment of locally baked pastries. Those who wanted an extensive menu frequented The Waffle House or Denny's up on the highway.

Cooper said, "You're not late Connie - just six thirty now. I opened a little early because Tom was pressing his nose against the glass when I got here, barely gave me time to brew the coffee."

She smiled and squeezed Tom's shoulder again, "How's it going Rev?"

"Fine, Connie," Tom lied.

Cooper broke six fresh eggs into a bowl and began to whisk them while he monitored the other items on the grill. Then he heated some olive oil in a pan and poured the eggs in and let them just set up before stirring in some of the grilled onions and a scoop of chopped portobello mushrooms.

As Tom sipped his coffee and glanced through his book. Cooper's mind was musing on the subject of Tom's troubles. Insomnia seemed an understandable response to his situation. Being a clergyman must be like being a stray dog at a whistler's convention.

Cooper slid the eggs onto warmed plates and added a generous portion of oven-roasted rosemary potatoes. He sat the plates on the counter and Connie whisked them off to the waiting couple. He felt once again that satisfying sense of hospitality that suffused his life here at The Happy Frog. He liked to think that people who wandered into the Frog found a sense of welcome that set their experience apart from that of a typical food place.

Turning his attention back to Tom, he said, "Tom, what's really keeping you awake."

Tom sighed. Did Cooper really want to know? He trusted Cooper and decided to take a chance, "Coop, I went to seminary because I had images of cloistered halls, spiritual journeys, awakened spirits, and a life of profound peace. Instead I was crammed full of pompous nonsense, archaic doctrine, and reasons "we" are superior to 'them.' Then I was asked to be a mid-level manager of a dysfunctional business selling a useless and outdated product. My colleagues turned out to be narcissistic twits, my superiors bloated bureaucrats, and my congregations full of people who know, at some level, they are being duped but don't know what to do about it other than distract themselves in petty spats and busy work."

Cooper whistled, "Lots of anger there, Tom. Better enjoy a nice breakfast before you have to preach a sermon this morning."

"No service on Christmas morning, Coop. We had a candlelight service last night and want people to be with their families this morning."

"And you?" Cooper asked.

"Doris and the kids are in Portland with the grandparents. I'll drive up later today."

"Lots of people coming by in a half hour or so," Cooper said, "Why don't you wait around and join us for a bit of holiday cheer?"

"What people?" Tom asked warily.

"Good people - Carl, Mary, Kathleen and Kogan Ito, Dorothy from the bookstore, Sam and Amy Hsu, Cap'n Phil - a few others."

Connie passed by with another pat on Tom's shoulders, "It's Christmas, Tom, you should stay and be with people who love you."

Tom looked at Cooper, who raised his eyebrows and whispered, "I'd suggest you not argue."

On the Wednesday after Christmas the western light was gradually beginning to linger in the evenings. Storms still battered their way along the coastline with sustained 80-90 mph winds, but breaks in the weather pattern were becoming a bit more frequent. This evening the sky was grey-black with low clouds, but there was a clear strip along the horizon in which the sun lingered for a moment before slipping behind the sea. As it lingered, it turned the underside of the clouds, for a brief moment, into a fiery vault. Cooper felt as if he were looking down on a field of lava. It lasted only an instant before the light faded and the starless darkness began.

Cooper stood up and went inside. He poured water into the kettle and set it on the burner, then scooped a spoon of Secret Valley Tea into his small hand-crafted cast iron brewing pot, a souvenir of his days in Okinawa. A pot such as this, purchased in the United States today, would cost several hundred dollars. The cast iron would keep the tea hot for an hour or two, time enough for a relaxed conversation.

He pulled the low table into the center of the room and placed two cushions beside it. He was just setting out a plate of small cinnamon scones when Tom Morton knocked at the door.

"Hello, Tom, please come in."

"Hi, Coop, thanks for sparing the time."

"No problem. It's a pleasure to visit with you. We don't get much chance to relax and talk."

Tom hung his coat on the bamboo rack by the door, then slipped off his shoes and laid them in on the small shelf. The entrance to Cooper's cottage was two-tier. The first small porch, just inside the front door, was about six feet wide, floored in polished wood, and ran the length of the cottage. It's walls were arrayed with hooks and shelves for tools, outerwear, and other items. A sliding shoji screen door led from this small porch to the interior of the cottage which was floored with tatami mats.

"Make yourself comfortable, Tom," Cooper gestured to the cushions. "The water is boiling and we'll have some tea." He took the cast iron brewing pot to the stove and carefully poured the hot water. He set the pot on the table by the scones and brought out two small ceramic cups. Seating himself across from Tom he took a breath, "This is a visit with a purpose, I think," he said to Tom.

"Cooper, I need to make some changes or I'll go insane. Let me ask you," he leaned forward, "are you an believer?"

Cooper's eyebrows raised, "That is a loaded term, Tom. What do you mean by, 'believer?'"

"Someone who believes in the existence of God."

Cooper shook his head. "It's hard to either affirm or deny the existence of something that can't be defined. What about you, Tom, are you an believer?"

"I think so," Tom said with and expression and tone of voice that implied great shame in such an admission, "but, honestly, Cooper, I want to know what you believe first."

"Define 'god' for me and I'll tell you whether or not I believe in it."

"Well," began Tom, "... the God of the Bible."

"That god," Cooper nodded, "No, I don't believe in that god for a moment. Outside of a few isolated verses, that god is a narcissistic, petty, vindictive, megalomaniac - not worthy of a second thought, let alone belief. The abusive chief of a primitive tribe."

Tom sat back and smiled, "Well, Cooper, come on, don't hold back. Tell me what you really think."

Cooper sighed, "Tom, you've raised a topic that people tend to dance around, tiptoe as if walking on egg shells, afraid to offend anyone's sensibilities. I'm not going to do that. There is too much bullshit piled up around this topic already."

Tom took a deep breath. "Coop, my job is to present this God in a winning manner, to come to the defense of the Bible and the God of the Bible. How can I effectively do that?"

"You can't, Tom. The god of the Bible is indefensible."

"Is there a God worthy of defense?"

Again Cooper smiled, "Any god worthy of defense would certainly neither need nor want defending."

"Let me repeat my first question, Coop, are you a believer of any sort?"

Cooper picked up the tea pot and poured the steaming liquid into the two cups. He picked up a scone. "Have some tea and scones, Tom. Let's not talk for just a few minutes." He bit into the scone and relaxed back onto his cushion.

Tom frowned, then nodded, and picked up his cup and sipped the tea while his thoughts raced round in circles.

Cooper broke the silence. "I'm sorry, Tom. I'm getting into word games with you. That might not be helpful. The direct answer to your question is, no, of course I'm not a believer by all common definitions of that word. I don't believe in any of the gods of religions. That doesn't mean that there isn't an "energy" and "intelligence" if you will, within the fabric of the Cosmos.

"But," he continued, "we can't talk about any energy or intelligence worthy of the spell symbol, G.O.D., without being tragically mistaken and delusional. My own experience of this Mystery is simply that of keeping my eyes and my mind open to the direct experience of the moment. That's where Whatever or Whomever can be encountered, nowhere else at all."

"So," Tom asked, "It boils down to, what you see is what you get?"

Cooper thought a moment, "Yes... but that means that we need to see as much as possible, both with our eyes and with our heart, our intuition. You know Connie, don't you?"

Tom nodded.

"I sense," said Cooper, "that Connie 'sees' a broader spectrum of reality than I do."

Tom nodded again.

"But if you were to ask Connie if she believed in God, can you guess what she'd answer?"

"No," Tom said, beginning to smile again.

"She'd pat you on the head and say, '*Your so sweet, dear,*' then go about her business.

"I suppose she would," Tom said.

Cooper took another sip of tea. "I know Connie's secret. She's never actually talked with me about it because she knows such talk is meaningless, but I do know her secret nonetheless."

"Really?" Tom asked, "what is it?"

"Connie," Cooper said, "is one of those people who knows, knows deep in her being, that she, herself, is part of God, as is all the rest of life. In order to know that, one *must* be a non-believer. Belief must be set aside because it blocks direct experience. Only a non-believer can truly be still enough to know God."

Tom sat quietly, feeling something begin to loosen in his chest. He sipped his tea and, for the first time that evening, actually tasted it. "You know, Coop, there's a passage in the Bible that says, 'be still and know that I am God.' Maybe it means that one *has* to be still in order to know God."

"One has to be still in order to know *anything*," Cooper replied.

Stillness descended on the cottage as the two men sipped their tea.

Chapter 16 - Breathe

"You are holding the brush as if it were trying to escape from your hand," Sam Hsu softly told Carl. "You are a skilled artist. Just because you are doing something unfamiliar does not mean that you must try harder or expend more effort."

Carl smiled and laid his brush down on the ceramic brush rest. He stepped away from the bench and stretched his arms above his head. "I wouldn't have thought it was so hard to make a series of simple strokes with the brush," he said.

Sam was quiet for a moment. His gaze rested on the calligraphy characters Carl had just painted. "I think maybe you are trying to do them correctly. Might that be the problem?"

"I shouldn't do them correctly?" Carl asked.

Sam kept his eyes on the rice paper and ink. "No," he shook his head, "Trying to be correct is to be incorrect. Do you understand?"

"I could say, 'yes,' but it would be a lie," Carl said. "Shouldn't I be trying to follow the rules of the strokes until I get them right and only then allow myself to expand and modify the form?"

"Some would say that," Sam replied, "but I would not agree. I think much time is wasted searching for perfection." He thought for a moment, then looked at Carl and said, "Let's take a walk together and let our minds unwind a bit."

The rain had tapered to a soft mist and the wind had died completely as they walked out on the campus of Williams University. The campus architecture was integrated with the surrounding forest in such a way that no building particularly stood out. Even the impressive Bartholomew Library spread its wings beneath a canopy of fir, cedar, and redwood trees and hid itself behind multiple layers of ferns and shrubs.

The two men walked in a companionable silence. Students ventured out from beneath their umbrellas and enjoyed the refreshing afternoon air. To Carl, the campus seemed soft, having no sharp edges and displaying countless hues of green and brown.

"I sometimes wish I could capture the feeling of the muted colors we see around us," Carl said as they turned onto the forest path that circled the campus.

Sam cocked his head and looked at him. "You want to paint these colors because you want to distract yourself from the discomfort you feel right now with your sumi painting. You think to yourself, 'maybe if I tried something else I would do better.' Is that not right?"

Carl felt a momentary defensiveness, but when he looked into Sam's open face he saw only authenticity and good will. His defensive urge quickly dissipated and he sighed. "You're probably right. I feel stuck and restless. I'm used to art coming naturally and easily. The Chinese calligraphy is something that doesn't follow that pattern and it's causing me to tense up, to try too hard."

"Yes," Sam nodded his head, "you are much too tight. You are trying much too hard. Here," he said, pointing to a small glade of Redwoods just off the trail, "we'll stop here and breathe for a bit."

A wooden bench sat at one edge of the glade, damp with the rain and mist. Sam brushed it off with his hands and laid his jacket on it. "Take off your jacket," he said to Carl, "then stand here quietly and see if you can feel the chi of the forest and the sky."

Sam stood with his feet about a shoulder's width apart and rested his hands over his abdomen, breathing naturally and quietly. He kept his eyes open but his gaze was relaxed. "Stand like this," he said, "and let your eyes be soft and able to see all around you without focusing on any one thing. Be aware of as much of the surrounding life as you can. Breathe softly but fully."

Carl took a deep breath and stood as directed. He noticed that he was concentrating on trying to breathe correctly. Sam noticed it immediately and said, "Do not try to breathe. Notice your breath, then forget it. Each thing you notice, notice it, then forget it completely. Leave space for the next noticing. Do not hold on to any thought or idea or image. Let it all flow through you like a river."

After five minutes, Sam asked Carl to begin moving his arms in a slow gentle rising and falling motion, initiating the movement from his waist in a flowing graceful pattern. "Follow my movements for the moment," Sam instructed, "When you feel your center, begin to move to your own rhythm."

They stood together in the misty coolness of the Redwood grove. "Let your arms rise and fall without effort," Sam said quietly, "as if they are being lifted and lowered on a cushion of air instead of pulled and pushed by muscles and tendons."

Carl closed his eyes for a moment and imagined his arms moving without muscle tension. He was surprised at how little effort was required for the wave-like up and down motion. He let his waist relax and noticed the connection between the center of his abdomen and the movement of his arms. He opened his eyes and let his waist and arms continue to move of their own accord. He lost track of time and was surprised when Sam gently said, "Now let your movement slow and return to stillness."

Carl's body came to rest, but he felt the flow of energy throughout his body continue to gently rise and fall. He looked over at Sam and smiled. Sam nodded and said, "Shall we walk back to the studio?"

Sam had a two-hour seminar to conduct, and he asked Carl to remain working in the studio until he returned and practice copying two characters. "What do these mean?" Carl asked.

Sam smiled and said, "I will tell you when I return. You just relax and let your body lead your mind."

Carl calmly cut a roll of rice paper into six-inch squares and began to copy the two characters. His fingers remained loose on the brush and his arms moved without effort as he let the black strokes appear on the white paper. As soon as he finished one sheet, he set it aside without thought and began a new one. He was still working when Sam returned.

"Have you been painting all this time," Sam asked.

Carl looked up, surprised, "Yes. How long have you been gone?"

"Two hours."

"Two hours? I don't believe it."

Sam smiled and looked at the sheets of rice paper piles and scattered about the table. "Do you have some you like?" he asked.

Carl stretched and reached across the table to a small pile of four or five sheets. "I like these. What do you think?"

Sam looked at him. "It doesn't matter what I think. Do you like them?"

Carl took a deep breath, "Yes, I like them."

Sam laughed and slapped Carl on the shoulder, "So do I."

Carl began to clean up his brushes and gather the scattered paper. "So, what do the characters mean?"

"They represent, 'wu-wei'" Sam replied, "It means 'act without effort.'"

They both turned as they heard a knock on the studio door.

A young woman opened the door. "I'm sorry, Sam. I didn't know you were busy."

"It's all right, Amy," Sam smiled, "come in and meet my friend Carl, Carl, this is my little sister, Amy."

Amy entered the room as Carl's eyes widened. She was a small woman, perhaps five feet four inches tall. Her short black hair framed her equally black eyes, eyes that crinkled in a smile as she extended her hand, "Carl, it seems like I know you. I hear about you a lot from Sam, Mr. Cooper, and Kathleen. I work for Kathleen, you know."

Carl took her hand and she gripped his own firmly, but warmly. She was in uniform and his mind flitted briefly and embarrassingly to repressed fantasies which he quickly dismissed. "It's nice to meet you, Amy," he smiled. *Amy! She would be named Amy,"* he mused.

Chapter 17 - Party

Winter, normally a grouchy ill-mannered tyrant on the Oregon coast, occasionally bestows a boon. This evening was one of them. The western horizon was free of fog and the breeze gentle enough to allow upright walking along the beaches and cliff edges. Carl's mood was relaxed and light, not just because of the gift of a beautiful day. He had spent the Christmas holidays, for the first time in his life, not with family and church, but with friends whose lives were open, accepting, and loving. He had feared that the season would bring renewed visits from depression and remorse, his life-long companions who had been in hiding the past few weeks. Instead he found a sense of hope and optimism even when the clouds, wind, and rain arrived.

The day passed quickly with a brisk business of book buyers and even a few art customers. One of Sam Hsu's scrolls sold at a price of $2,500, causing Carl to whistle as Dot showed him the check. "I can't imagine ever selling a painting for that much money."

"Why not, Carl? Some of Sam's work goes for five times that price."

"I know. But I'm sure not Sam."

"I know. You're Carl. Sam is a tall Chinese man. So?"

"Well, Sam is a master painter."

"What would Sam say if you called him a 'master painter?'"

Carl laughed. "He would say that we were both beginners."

"That's what he would say indeed," Dorothy said, "and I'd like to be around when you sell a painting for that amount, right here in this store."

After closing the store they sat in one of the art alcoves and ate some bread, cheese, and fruit while sharing a pot of Snow on Bamboo tea, relaxing while waiting for Sam Hsu to come by and give them a ride to an evening gathering at the home of Kenny and Paul.

"How old are you, Dot?" Carl asked out of the blue.

"Well, young man, that's an impertinent question," Dot smiled.

Carl laughed, "Well, consider the source."

"I"m forty-seven," she replied as she sipped her tea.

"When I first met you, you know, that day you hired me? I thought you were about thirty."

Dot looked up and smiled coyly, "My how you do flirt."

Carl stammered, "Oh, no, I didn't mean…"

"Carl," Dot said, "I'm teasing. You're curious about me and my life. That's natural. I'm curious about your background as well, but your background is not who you are. My curiosity is simply, well… just curiosity."

"Yeah," Carl nodded, "You're a friend and a fascinating woman. I'm not flirting, just curious."

He took a bite of cheese and a sip of tea and continued, "Do you enjoy living alone?"

"I enjoy living by myself, but I don't live alone. I live in the midst of friends. I live close to many people who love me; one who loves me very much."

"Cooper?"

"Cooper and I love each other. We have each been living by ourselves for many years and we don't envision that changing. But just because you live by yourself doesn't mean you live alone or live without love. Do you understand what I mean?"

"I think so," Carl said, "I'm thousands of miles from everything familiar to me. I'm not in a relationship with a woman for the first time since college. I don't know where I'm headed or what I'm going to do. Yet…"

"Yet?" Dot asked

"Yet I've never felt more supported and encouraged. Everything I thought I knew about friendship is changing. In a few months I'm closer to more people in a real way than I've ever been with my old 'friends.' I don't think about Amy at all, and I was engaged to her for Pete's sake!"

"Amy?" Dot looked startled.

"Amy back home," Carl smiled, "not Amy Hsu."

"Well," said Dot, "that's a relief. I don't think entering into a relationship with a State Trooper is the best thing for you right at the moment. Though…" she considered for a moment, "… you never can tell."

At that moment Sam Hsu knocked on the window of the front door, smiling and gesturing for them to hurry. Amy stood just behind him.

Cooper sat in the leather armchair, sipped 16 year old Lagavulin Scotch, and contemplated the ocean through the floor-to-ceiling window in the living room of Paul and Kenny's elegant yet comfortable Otter Rock home. The sky was clear and a full moon cast a strip of light along the surface of the water all the way to the horizon. Kenny and Connie were sitting in the dining area to his right, arguing over the merits of Mercier's *Night Train to Lisbon.* Mary and Kathleen were having a sisterly conference on the redwood patio just outside. Ito was helping Paul create something in the kitchen that wafted a tantalizing aroma throughout the house.

It was a lovely evening. He was sitting in luxury, surrounded by ocean and forest, in the company of people he loved. He was also mired in a melancholic mood that seemed to deepen each day as the winter slowly ebbed. Melancholia was his own version of early spring fever. When others were putting forth the buds of new optimism and energy with the coming of longer days, he was withdrawing into sadness and nameless longing.

He heard the doorbell ring and a bustle of conversation at the other end of the room. Another sigh accompanied the feeling that he should get up and greet the new arrivals. He ignored the feeling and savored another sip of the single malt Scotch from the Isle of Islay. Even this luxury contributed to his mood as he reflected that the lovely wind-swept distillery on the coast of Islay was now owned by Diageo, a multi-billion dollar international company with offices in over eighty countries. *Kenny's money is flowing, like all money does, to the top,* he mused. Another sigh. *Enough,* he thought and rose to meet his friends.

Sam Hsu had arrived along with his sister Amy, Carl, and Dorothy. Cooper wondered if Carl's arrival with Sam and Amy indicated that a relationship with Amy was in the works? Cooper made the proper noises to everyone and then managed to slip in to the background again and retreat to his chair, his Scotch, and his mood.

Carl had indeed arrived with Sam and Amy, but there was no obvious match making involved. Sam had simply offered to give Carl and Dorothy a ride to the get-together. Kenny was in his usual gregarious host mood and was showing everyone to the snacks and drinks counter. Carl saw the bottle of Lagavulin and poured himself a "wee splash." His eyes drifted to the magnificent view and then to Cooper, sitting with his back to the room and his feet propped up in the recliner. He wondered about this. Just a moment ago Cooper had greeted him and then disappeared. Cooper was never the center of attention, but he seemed to always be available, a solid presence in the midst of whatever conversation was going on. He took his glass and walked over to the window and sat down in the matching leather chair beside Cooper.

Cooper smiled a welcome but was silent, so Carl remained silent as well. He thought for a moment that he should respect the silence and return to the others, but Cooper then turned to him and said, gesturing to the view, "The world can be a lovely place, can't it?" His words were appreciative but Carl caught a dark tinge in his tone of voice.

"It is lovely," he responded, "but, truthfully Coop, you sound as if you're not in a particularly lovely mood. What's up?"

Cooper turned back to the window and was silent.

"Sorry, I didn't mean to pry," Carl said as he started to get up.

"No, Carl," Cooper turned to him, "please sit down. Let me tell you a bit about myself. No sense sitting here letting my mood spoil a gorgeous evening and an expensive Scotch."

Carl nodded and sat back down, "It is a wonderful Scotch. I'm continually surprised at the changes in myself. Six months ago I had never tasted Scotch and never seen the Pacific Ocean."

Cooper smiled, "Things change, don't they?"

"They sure do."

Cooper tasted the Scotch again, "Mmm, yes, this is very good. I've been sitting here in a mood and not appreciating it."

"Is something wrong?" Carl asked.

Cooper folded down the foot rest and stretched his legs. He sat forward in the chair and turned a bit to face Carl. "No, nothing's wrong…" he paused and chuckled, "… well, in fact, everything's wrong… and there's nothing really wrong with that. It's just that sometimes the beauty of my surroundings and the dearness of my life serves to remind me of how transient it all is. It will all disappear in a moment."

Carl sat back, "Wow, OK, other than that, Mrs. Lincoln, how do you like the play?"

Cooper's eyes twinkled, "The play is wonderful. Sometimes the acting sucks."

They both looked again to the ocean. Cooper's eyes misted. "Carl," he said, "I feel powerless. I know that the steamroller we have ironically called 'civilization' is going to flatten everything I love. In one sense, that's OK. Everything ends, and begins again. But I'm apparently going to have to watch as it happens. I don't think there is a Frodo who can save us. The One Ring is already in the hands of the Dark Lord."

Cooper leaned back in his chair again. "I'm sorry, Carl. I'm not very good company, but don't worry about me. This too will pass."

Carl felt a hand on his shoulder and looked up into Dot's smiling eyes.

"Need you in the kitchen for a moment, Carl. Do you mind?"

As they walked to the kitchen where everyone had gathered to watch Paul work his magic with salmon, Dot squeezed Carl's arm and he stopped and asked her, "Is Cooper OK?"

Dot nodded. "He's fine, Carl. He just sometimes feels things very intensely."

Carl shook his head, "It's just that I've always pictured him as the model of serenity; a person who really 'has it together.'"

"He's seen many things come and go, Carl. He truly is, as you say, 'together,' but a key part of being 'together' is feeling an authentic sadness, depression if you will, at the unnecessary pain and misery humanity brings to itself. He knows he can't change it or fix it, and that the only thing to do is to live his life as creatively and lovingly as possible, but he has to feel his sorrow on a regular basis. We all do. Life is a beautiful tragedy in which we get to act all the parts."

Just then applause filled the kitchen as Paul, a triumphant smile on his face, pulled a salmon roast from the oven and placed it on the counter. Glasses were raised in a toast to the chef. Carl glanced back and saw Cooper standing in the kitchen doorway, his own glass raised and his eyes glistening with tears.

We get to act all the parts, Carl thought to himself.

Chapter 18 - Campout

Something screamed in the distance, mimicking a woman in mortal peril. Goosebumps sprang up on Dot's skin and she looked across the campfire to where Cooper sat with a cup of chocolate. Kathleen sat to his right and Ito was cleaning up the dinner dishes in a basin over by the tents. Cooper smiled at her. "Fox," he said.

"Really?" she said, "How could such a small animal make such a large sound? It gives me shivers," she continued, "how much like a human scream of agony it sounded. I wonder what it meant to the fox."

"A mating call?" ventured Cooper.

"Mary would know what it meant," said Ito, "I wish she and Connie could have come along."

"Actually," Cooper said, "they're delighted to stay with the Happy Frog. It's very much their home still, even though I'm technically the owner. Connie's never happier than when she's taking care of customers. They're her family."

"I've known her for decades," Kathleen said, "and I still don't really know what makes her tick. Mary doesn't volunteer much about their private life. I mean, I love Connie, but she has a veil of mystery about her."

"She's a fairy Queen who has decided to spend some time among humans," Ito said. Everyone smiled at his words while thinking to themselves, *Could be.*

Kathleen, Ito, Cooper, and Dot were celebrating the first night of a long-planned and long-awaited getaway to the Mt. Hood Wilderness. Weather was always an iffy thing in early April, but early spring was also a time when the forest was at its peak of fecundity. A hundred shades of green surrounded them as they drove up Highway 26 into the National Forest.

They arrived at the campground early in the afternoon and found a semi-isolated spot to establish their tents and relax into the evening. Other campers were scattered through the campground, but the sites were well designed to give each one a bit of privacy. Some amenities such as toilets and clean water were necessary for the trip. As Kathleen had said, "This is not a survival trek or vision quest, this is a family campout. We are going to a *nice* campground!"

"She has a lit. degree and they have a wonderful library," Cooper added. "Have you noticed that it contains only hard cover volumes, some of them quite lovely?"

"Yes," Dot said, "and only *good* books, in the true meaning of the word. No best-sellers cranked out by a formula combining lawyers, cops, murder, and sex."

"What is a good book," Cooper asked the group, "how would you classify a book as good? I mean *really* good; worth having a hard back copy in your library; something you'd read over and over and wouldn't hesitate to recommend to a close friend?" He turned to Dot, "You're the bookseller, how do you choose a good book?"

Dot groaned, "Ouch, Coop. That's a loaded question for me. As a person, I know what I consider to be a good book. As a bookseller, however, I get caught in the intricacies of marketing, publishing, and societal norms; all of which have little to do with quality literature. A 'good book' is one that people buy."

"So a best-seller is not necessarily a good book, then?" Ito questioned.

"Ack!" Dot made a choking motion with her finger to her mouth, "I've never, or hardly ever, seen a best-selling book that I would call a good book by Cooper's criteria. And the term, 'best-selling' is bullshit as well. A book doesn't become a best-seller because lots of people buy it. They buy it because it is called a 'best-seller.' And the quality of the writing has very little to do with it. It's the formula, the hype and the author's name that set the standard."

"Pretty cynical view for someone who sells books," Cooper teased.

"There is a cynical edge there," admitted Dot, "but I also love good books and I give minimum attention to the bullshit and maximum attention to lovely books. You know that Coop," she admonished Cooper.

"I do," said Cooper, "And you've created a wonderful center for books. You have a small section of best sellers by the counter, but when you step farther into the store you enter a world of, what I would call, *good* books of all sorts."

Dot got up and walked around the campfire and kissed Cooper on the forehead. "Thank you, Coop. I love what I do." She sat beside him and hooked her arm around his, snuggling closer in the chill of the evening.

"Back to the question," Kathleen said, "do good books have to be serious books, full of angst and human drama?"

Ito answered, "There are good books of every type, I think. For instance there are children's classics that would have to be called 'good' - even from a strict literary definition. All good books do, however, deal in some way with the human condition whether in drama, humor, fable, or poetry, don't they?"

Cooper said, "I'd include that in my criteria. A good book doesn't just entertain or distract. It can be entertaining and distracting, but it would have to be more than that to be in Connie's library I think."

Dot added, "And it has to be pleasant to read. Not in the happy sense, but the way the words and sentences are constructed must be pleasing in some manner. The very act of reading, not just the story, must be compelling."

Kathleen asked, "Dot, what good books are you reading right now?"

The conversation continued long into the cold spring night.

A gentle pre-dawn rain sounded against the tarp that sheltered the table and fire pit as Cooper spooned coffee into the press-pot. No "cowboy coffee" for him. A man who brews coffee for a living does not come unprepared on a camping trip. Besides, a press-pot is the most efficient and natural way of brewing coffee, even in the semi-wilderness of an Oregon State Park. No one else was stirring. Last night's conversation had continued until late, as everyone relaxed into the glow of the fire and the spaciousness that comes from being out from under a roof and in the safety of loving company.

The kettle on the cast iron grill that laid across the morning fire was boiling. Cooper removed it and set it on the table to let the boil settle for a moment, then poured a bit into the press-pot, stirred it with a wooden spoon, then filled the pot with the hot water. He placed the lid on the pot then took the kettle and walked through the drizzle of rain to the water container and filled it, brought it back and set it on the grill to boil again. One pot of coffee was not enough for this crew of coffee connoisseurs, especially in the appetite-stimulating mountain morning.

"Coop, you out there," Dot said, peering out of the tent flap of their two-person tent tucked between two fir trees.

"Just making coffee," he replied.

"Come here for a minute, would you?" she asked.

He walked over to the tent. "What?" he asked.

"Come in the tent for a minute," she said, moving back into the darkness.

"Why? The coffee's just about ready."

"This won't take long," she replied.

"Oh! Well... I like strong coffee anyway." He quickly ducked into the tent and into her arms.

"Quietly," she whispered.

"I'm not going to scream," he whispered back, "but be gentle with me, I'm just a lad."

"Excellent coffee, Coop," Ito said as he sat in the folding camp chair and sipped from a mug.

"Thanks. I let it brew a bit longer than usual, just as an experiment."

"A successful one," added Kathleen, savoring her own steaming mug.

"I think so myself," Cooper said, with a smile of appreciation.

Light was stealing into the campground as the rain stopped, the sun rose, and the clouds began to part. "Maybe we'll have a Camelot week here," Dot mused as she stood and took a deep breath of the forest air.

"Camelot week?" Ito puzzled.

"The rain may never fall till after sundown" Kathleen sang, "by eight the morning fog must disappear… here in Camelot."

Dot laughed and patted Ito's shoulder, "It's a song from an old musical, Camelot. It's such a magical kingdom that the weather has to obey certain rules, like raining only at night."

Everyone moved their chairs out into a patch of morning sun, refiled their coffee, sat and stretched out their legs with contented sighs. "You're quiet, Cooper-san," Ito said, "are you thinking about the day ahead?"

"No, not really," Cooper said, "I'm happy at the moment not to think of anything past this moment, this cup of coffee, and the blessings of friends." He lifted his cup in a salute. "In fact, I think I'll spend the day right here with a book; take a morning nap, read some more, have some lunch, then an afternoon nap, more reading, a drink or two, dinner, and a nap before bed. You guys run along and be intrepid hikers. I'm too old."

Dot coughed and choked a bit on her coffee, "All evidence to the contrary," she said. "Come, Kathleen, walk to the showers with me and we'll talk girl talk while Coop fixes breakfast."

Cooper and Ito watched the women stroll down the trail to the old concrete shower house. Ito shook his head and gave a wistful sigh, "You know, my friend, how dangerous it is to love so much in a world as ephemeral as this."

"Yes," Cooper nodded, "I know. But the alternative of not loving does not protect us, it deadens us. The transient nature of it all makes it all the more beautiful. It's a world of happy tears, my friend."

"Yes," smiled Ito, "Happy tears."

"I was thinking about your man, Ed Abbey, this morning," Dot said to Cooper as they walked hand-in-hand along a forest service road winding its way up to a fire lookout. "He spent quite a few summers in a lookout like the one we're heading for, I think."

"My man Ed Abbey?" Cooper laughed, "What makes Ed Abbey, 'my man?'"

Dot squeezed his hand. "I just sense that he is an alter-ego for you. He's your shadow side."

"Shadow?"

"Not shadow in the bad or evil sense, but in the sense that he embodies qualities that you have but don't acknowledge, at least not consciously."

"Tell me more about this shadow of mine," Cooper said, a bit of an edge to his voice.

"Coop," Dot shook her head, "I'm not psychoanalyzing you. I'm just projecting onto you what I sense from reading Abbey. You have the same passion, even the same anger, but you have smoother edges than Abbey."

"Smoother edges. Is that a good thing?"

The forest service road made a sharp turn to the left and began a steep climb. From where they were, they could see it switch back and forth several times as it made its way up to the top of the rise. They paused before turning up the road and Cooper turned to Dot.

"Is smoother good?" he asked again.

"I love your edges, Coop," she put her arms around his neck and kissed him softly. "Smooth is very good." She kept her arms around his neck and looked at him for a moment. "You have Abbey's anger and outrage and I don't want it to turn inward on your heart, that's all."

Cooper sighed, "All the years I spent at the retreat center, living essentially a monastic life, gave me a sense of contentment that I didn't think I could ever lose." He took her hand and they continued up the road. "Coming to Carson Beach and The Happy Frog was a good decision. I've been happy and satisfied."

"But?" Dot said, looking ahead up the road.

"But," he said, "there has been an exponential increase in the madness of society in the past ten years, and it's not just in my perspective. It's real and measurable by any objective standard. We're coming apart at the seams."

They continued in silence for a few hundred yards. The road switched back again and the sun poked through the branches, warming the climb.

"And," Cooper sighed again, "I feel a sense of futility. I guess you could say I feel impotent."

"All evidence to the contrary," she said as she snuggled against his arm.

Cooper chuckled, "Yes, there's that. Thank you ma'am. But you're right. I think Ed Abbey was angry because he sensed his own impotency in the face of what he saw happening to the American West. He could rant and rail against it. He could write, *The Monkey Wrench Gang*, to express his feelings. But he couldn't stop the bulldozer."

Dot said, "Barbara Kingsolver used to live near him in Arizona. She wrote that once he took his television out in his back yard and shot it with his shotgun."

"That happened more than once," Cooper said, then added, "That must have been a satisfying feeling."

"Would you like to blast your television, if you had a shotgun; or for that matter if you had a television?" Dot asked.

They walked in silence again for a moment. Then Cooper said, "Yes. I would enjoy something like that. You think I should go buy a television and a shotgun?"

"I think you would benefit from doing something wild and crazy."

"Some would say I've lived a rather wild and crazy life already," Cooper replied. "Certainly my parent's died thinking I was crazy as a loon for, in their words, 'wasting a perfectly good law degree.'"

"That's not what I mean," Dot said. "I'm not sure what I mean, Coop. I don't mean to sound as if you should be different from who you are. I love who you are. It's just that walking up to the lookout made me think of Ed Abbey and of your appreciation of his life and words."

The road made one final switchback and they emerged onto a treeless summit. The wooden framework of the observation tower rose three stories to a platform that supported a square building whose windows afforded a 360 degree panorama of the forest.

"Let's climb up and see if Ed is home," Cooper said.

They stood on the deck that ran along all four sides of the building and looked in silence at the majestic cone of Mt. Hood. It was white-clad, but they knew that its snow pack was a fraction of its usual winter accumulation. It had been the driest winter on record.

Cooper noticed that the beauty of the vista coexisted with his own anger and sadness. Dot was right, he would benefit from some outlet for the energy that was building up within him. His runs on the beach were refreshing. His work as a cook was creative and satisfying. He had loving relationships. But the accumulated repression of his anger and dismay at the ignorance of his society was becoming unhealthy, beginning to contaminate these other elements of his life.

He filed this awareness away in his mind and turned his attention fully to the place, the time, and the person he was with. He put his arm around Dot, nuzzled her hair, and said softly, "I love you."

It was twilight by the time they returned to the campground. Ito was cooking a pot of seasoned rice over the grill and getting ready to lay skewers of vegetables and fresh shrimp alongside the rice pot. The evening was soft and the sounds from adjoining campsites were muted.

"Welcome back," Ito said.

Kathleen added, "where have you two been all day?"

"Visiting a friend of Cooper's," Dot replied.

Chapter 19 - You Never Know

"How was the vacation," Carl asked as he sat down at the counter where Cooper was grinding coffee for the first brewing of the morning. The cafe had not opened yet, but Carl was now in the habit of showing up early, knowing that Cooper or Connie would be glad to let him into the warmth of the Happy Frog for conversation, coffee, and some extra help with the set-up preparations.

"Lovely," Cooper said, then started the burr-grinder and paused as its grinding noise filled the morning quiet. When the coffee was ground he continued, "We honestly felt like we were in another world, a world of natural peace and joy"

"Really," Carl smiled, "You must have hated to come back."

"I'm happy to be here this morning," Cooper said as he started the coffee brewer, then asked Carl, "Want some press-pot coffee? I've got a pot in the kitchen."

"Thanks," Carl said and followed Cooper into the kitchen where Connie was stirring the oatmeal that was bubbling in a large kettle. She looked up from her task and held up the long wooden spoon and waved it at Carl. She cackled in a hoarse voice, "Double, double, toil and trouble. Fire burn and caldron bubble."

"Eye of Newt oatmeal, my favorite," Carl laughed.

"Don't encourage her," Cooper said, rolling his eyes.

"Ah, you'll be sorry, my pretty," Connie cackled at Cooper.

"You're mixing your stories," Cooper said as he took the spoon from her and returned it to the kettle. "Your in the land of Oz now."

"I knew it wasn't Kansas," she said, "now where'd I put the frog's toes?"

"She gets in these moods now and then," Cooper shook his head and took Carl's arm, "Let's go set up the tables before she turns us into actual happy frogs."

They left the kitchen while Connie continued to stir the oatmeal, singing, "Round about the cauldron go…"

As Carl was bustling about the cafe, setting out tableware and pottery vases of flowers, he was humming to himself.

"Good mood this morning?" Cooper asked as he sliced tomatoes on the cutting board behind the counter.

"Yes," Carl replied, "very good."

Carl had become a steady, if unpaid, helper during the breakfast hours at the Happy Frog. He wasn't due at Words and Images until 10:00 AM on most days and the relaxed community at the cafe was an essential part of his life. On his two days off each week he would wander the coast, on foot or in his old Mazda, and find places to sketch. The weathered trees and sculpted rocks of the coast were his primary subjects. He would sketch for a day, then use his sketches to inspire his paintings. Most of his painting was done in the evenings, a time when he would sublimate the childhood anxious feelings that arose as darkness deepened and let the energy flow through his brush instead of creating stories in his mind.

Last night he had produced one of those paintings that seemed to happen only by accident, emerging from this arm and brush with little effort and no conscious planning. Within a few minutes he had the outline of a twisted cedar tree clinging to a bit of soil on the face of a cliff. It was a good image. He would work on it a bit more tonight, taking care not to add too much; a branch here and a background shade there. One extraneous stroke could ruin the effect that he saw emerging.

"Any particular reason?" Cooper followed.

"I enjoyed painting last night… and, well, I think of my life."

"Your life?"

"Less than a year ago I was living in Grand Rapids, teaching at a

Christian High School, and engaged to be married. I was nice, dependable, a bit of an underachiever according to my family, friends, and fiancé, but nevertheless one with good potential.

"Now I am living in a shack on the Oregon coast, working at a bookstore and painting. My community is actually a crazy little cafe and my friends are a cook, a Chinese artist, two lesbian women, one of whom could actually be a witch, a police lieutenant, a Japanese physician, a wild animal vet, and a bookseller.

"I have no career, no plans, no IRA, no bank accounts, and no religion. Coop, I've never felt so happy in my life!"

Cooper smiled at Carl and fell silent as if he were thinking of something far away.

"You are a lucky man, Carl, to have no plans. I had a briefcase full of plans when I was your age and it took me decades to be rid of them."

"What were your plans at my age, Coop?" Carl asked as he finished setting up the tables and came to sit at the counter where Coop was slicing and dicing.

"I'd finished law school and was getting out of the Air Force. I was going to be a successful attorney with a big firm in the city."

"City?" Carl asked.

"There's only one 'city' Carl; San Francisco," Cooper sniffed.

"Of course," Carl hurriedly agreed. "And...?"

Cooper shook his head and looked down at his chopping board, "You know a bit of my story, Carl. It seemed like every time I turned around I was losing something; jobs, wife, dreams; things just kept changing and, at the time, I didn't think they should change. They should stand still for awhile. Now," he smiled, "I know better. Now every day's an adventure. You are finding that out about 20 years earlier than I did, Carl. That's where you are so fortunate."

"Things will change for me too, I suppose," Carl said.

"Yes," Cooper pulled two mugs off the shelf and poured freshly brewed coffee into them and gave one to Carl and sighed, "things will change for you too." Then he shook his head and turned toward the front door. "Time to open up." he pointed toward the door, "Unlock it, my friend, but be careful. You never know what's going to come through the door when you open it in the morning."

Carl laughed and said, "Well, let's see." He unlocked the door and opened it, placing the wooden "Welcome" sign in its stand outside. He turned and walked back to the counter.

The door opened and the chimes jingled. He turned around and saw Amy Hsu walk in. She smiled and waved in his direction. He turned and looked at Cooper who rolled his eyes toward the ceiling, turned and walked into the kitchen, humming softly the theme from Twilight Zone, "Do do do do, do do do do…"

Amy was dressed in mufti rather than her State Police uniform. Carl noticed that her black hair curled around her neck in a Diane Keaton sort of way, if you could picture Diane Keaton as a diminutive Chinese woman in her late twenties. The last time he had seen Amy was at Paul and Kenny's party up in Otter Rock. He hadn't paid much attention. She was Sam's younger sister and Sam Hsu was his mentor, a man he respected, admired, and wanted to emulate. This morning, however, she was neither Sam's sister nor a State Trooper. She was a young woman with sparkling black eyes and clear olive skin. He wanted to talk to her.

"Hello Amy," he said in his best casual voice, "You're out early this morning."

"Hi Carl," she slipped off her jacket and hung it by the door. "I'm here because I'm hungry. I have the day off and I'm going to spend it doing nothing that I don't want to do and everything that comes to mind that I want to do," she blurted all in one breath, then stood looking somewhat sheepish. "I mean…"

Cooper stepped in from the kitchen. "How does scrambled eggs, with almond slivers, mushrooms, and shaved roasted zucchini sound?"

"Wonderful, Cooper," she said, "how did you know?"

Cooper paused, "Well… Connie told me."

"Figures," Carl said.

"How about you Carl," Cooper added, "have time for breakfast?"

"Uh, sure," Carl stammered.

"Good," Cooper said, "You two sit over by the window and I'll bring some coffee."

Amy and Carl looked at each other. Amy shrugged her shoulders. "Looks like we're having breakfast together," she said with a small smile. "Is that OK?"

Carl stood for a moment trying to figure out what was happening, Something was happening. A moment ago he was articulate and confident about his new rootless but happy life, now he was about to have breakfast with a young woman who as yet did not have a part in that life. He wasn't sure he was up for that. He recovered his voice just in time to head off the embarrassed silence. "Yes, that'd be nice," he said, and meant it.

"All right, witch woman," Cooper said as he stirred the shaved zucchini in a pan with a bit of olive oil, "they're sitting at the same table talking with each other and both looking like they're at a Junior High School dance. I hope you're satisfied."

"Cooper," Connie protested, "I just wanted Carl to have some breakfast before he left. You know I'm not a matchmaker."

Cooper snorted, "I remember some years ago when I ended up at a dinner table with a woman named Dorothy Waters. Everyone else seemed to disappear. Of course you had nothing to do with that."

"Of course not," Connie righteously lifted her chin and walked into the dining room to greet new customers whose entry had sounded the door chimes.

Cooper broke eggs into a bowl and began to whisk them. He wasn't sure about Connie's latest "sense of things." In his mind, Carl needed more time by himself and was not ready to be in a relationship with a woman. The more he whisked the eggs the more concerned he became. When Connie returned he spoke up. "Connie," he laid down the bowl and whisk and leaned on the counter, "do you really think this is a good thing for either Carl or Amy?"

Connie caught the concern in Cooper's voice and turned to face him. "Coop, I'm really not matchmaking in the true sense of the word. I'm really not. Both Carl and Amy have a good amount of time to spend on their own yet. But they each have qualities that would benefit the other person, they really do. They're not going to fall in love, but they each need the stimulation of a person their own age."

"Stimulation?"

"They each need an intimate friend to provide a place where they can explore some of the issues they avoid."

"Carl has friends," Cooper said, "good friends - me, you, Kathleen, Sam,..."

Connie cut him off. "Coop," she said, shaking her head, "we are good friends with him, but there is an intimacy that he won't find with us that is very important for him. It's very important for Amy too."

"A friend with privileges?" Cooper asked.

"Maybe," Connie shrugged, "maybe not, but trust me on this Cooper. They needed to have a little push in that direction or they each would keep on building subtle walls against deeper intimacy. They'll be good for each other, Coop. Maybe not as life partners but as friends - even with privileges."

Cooper thought for a moment, "OK, woman, I'll trust you. When have I not?" He remembered his own need of self-sufficiency as an antidote to the losses of his life; how that need began to extend beyond self-sufficiency into isolation without his noticing. It was Connie who gently re-introduced him to his need for a deeper intimacy with women. He smiled as he began to lightly brown the slivers of almonds in the oil. He still, after years in Carson Beach, thought about Connie and wondered, *Who, or what, IS this woman?*

Later that evening, after his stint at the bookstore, Carl met Amy at Mo's Chowder House on the waterfront for ale and chowder. As they sat and sipped their ale, Carl decided to broach a touchy subject, at least in his mind. "This is sort of strange," he said. "Amy is the name of my ex-fiancee, and here I am having beer and chowder with a woman named Amy."

Amy smiled, "Well, you don't have to worry about getting in trouble by using the wrong name in a moment of passion." She caught a hint of panic on Carl's face and quickly added, "I'm just kidding. Passion with you is the last thing on my mind." Carl's countenance took on yet a different expression and she stammered, "I mean... passion would be fine, but... oh, shit, I'll shut up now." She blushed deeply and took a sip of her ale.

Carl reached over and touched her arm, "I'm feel awkward too," he said. "I haven't gone on a date in years."

"Is this a date?" Amy cocked her head and gave him a grave look.

Carl felt a sense of warmth and caution. Amy seemed very vulnerable and he knew he didn't want to do or say anything to trespass on that vulnerability. Of course, he was probably projecting his own considerable vulnerability onto her. He looked at her and said, "I think it's a date. What do you think?"

She nodded her head and said softly, "I think it is a date..."

Chapter 20 - The Visitor

Carl marveled at the transformation that took place as Carson Beach readied itself for another Summer. Shop windows were washed, sidewalks scrubbed, crosswalk stripes repainted, and a general mood that seemed to contain an equal mix of excitement and dread. The excitement rested in the anticipation of a large inflow of income for shopkeepers, restaurateurs, hoteliers, fisherman, and just about every aspect of the shoreline economy. The dread rested in the fact that this influx of money was accompanied by an influx of...*people*. As Dorothy said one morning as she and Carl were unpacking a shipment of "what to do on the Oregon coast" type of books, "Why can't they just stay home and send us the money?"

The dependence on Summer tourism was a mixed blessing for those who called Carson Beach home - a group that now included Carl de Wilde. The tourist trade enabled the residents to live in reasonable economic comfort in an area that offered the wild beauty and solitude they cherished. It also shattered that beauty and solitude for a period of time. It was a trade-off, one that was met with a sometimes slightly grudging attitude, but mostly with good humor and hospitality.

Dorothy and Carl were doing their own bit to welcome the season by redoing the window displays at the *Words and Images* bookstore. Dot started the bookstore twenty years ago with very little capital and a belief that the minority of the American public that was both literate and appreciative of literature was at least large enough to support one bookstore on the coast that stocked good books.

Her connections with the Portland art world gave her enterprise the "plus" it needed to position it as having a character that separated it from mere eccentricity. The combination of fine art and fine literature turned out to be an attraction that brought customers from as far south as San Francisco and as far north as Victoria. She stocked books of high quality in both content and form, displayed them in a manner that invited browsing, and complimented this display with the work of carefully selected Northwestern artists. The combination brought her a degree of regional fame, and, if not fortune, at least a comfortable and satisfying life.

Carl thrived in the environment of *Words and Images.* His degree in Fine Arts was actually proving useful, contrary to the pessimistic warnings of his family. He earned enough at the bookstore to live a simple minimalist life-style that, at the moment, pleased him greatly. He had friendships of a sort that he had never before experienced. He had established a student relationship with one of the finest artists he had ever known. And he was immersed in his own work as an artist. Summer's arrival on the Oregon coast seemed appropriate for the warmth he found growing in himself.

As usual, Dorothy was already at the shop when he arrived a little before ten that morning. He unlocked the back door and entered the small hallway off of which were a small office, a bathroom, and a storage room.

"Morning Dot," he called out cheerfully.

"Morning Carl," he heard Dorothy call from the front of the store. "Coffee's on. Grab a cup, then come see what I've got."

He went in the office where the freshly brewed coffee aroma filled the small space. He took his mug from the hook and poured it half-full of the hot coffee, took a sip, and smiled. *I wonder what she's got.*

He walked up the long center aisle of the shop, feeling the warmth of the mug of coffee merge with the warmth of the shelves full of books. Each group of shelves was interspersed with an alcove in which hung carefully selected art work. *Wouldn't it be something,* he thought as he looked around, *if someday I had something hanging here?* He always carefully avoided any suggestion that he might sell his art here. Dorothy also avoided that subject. Each of them knew the time was not yet right for him to take that step. *Let it happen when it wants to happen,* he said to himself.

Dorothy was at the front counter carefully leafing through a small book. "Look," she said like a child showing off her favorite toy. She closed the book to reveal a brown cloth-bound cover. "My brother, Ted, found this in a box of our grandmother's books that he stored away in his attic without really looking at them. He just sent it to me." She smiled and gently let her finger run along the spine of the old book. Carl noticed that she wore her white cotton gloves, a sure sign that the book was special.

"What is it?" he asked, leaning forward to look for a title.

"It's a first edition of *Walden*," she whispered, "published in 1854 by Ticknor and Fields in Boston. My brother, bless his heart, said that I should have it seeing as I'm the bibliophile of the family." She sighed quietly, thoughts drifting to warm family memories tinged with melancholy.

"Lovely," Carl said, "was your grandmother a book person?"

"Sort of," Dot replied, "She wan't highly educated but she loved to read. She died when I was ten or eleven and I never really knew what she had in her small personal library. I didn't come to love books until later - high school and college. This must have been sitting in Ted's attic for at least thirty years."

Carl opened one of the drawers under the counter and found a pair of cotton gloves. He put them on and Dot handed him the book like she were offering him a treasure.

He let the book open naturally in his hands. "Not to be crass," he said, "but how much is it worth?"

"I haven't examined it carefully yet," she said, "but it has eight pages of the publisher's catalogue intact so I would imagine somewhere between ten and twenty thousand dollars."

Carl carefully laid the book back in Dot's hands. "Don't be afraid," she laughed, "you're not going to break it. I'll never sell it anyway, so it really doesn't matter what someone says it's worth in dollars."

"You can't just read it like an ordinary book, though," Carl said.

"No," she agreed, "it will have to be protected in a box. It's an heirloom, a work of art." She smiled and murmured, "Cooper will love this." She looked up. "It's time to open up. Let's put this in the back when it will be safe."

They walked to the back of the store. Dot carefully wrapped the book in a cloth and placed it in a desk drawer. Carl heard a light knock on the front door and looked toward the front of the store.

"Oh, my god," he whispered, "it's Amy."

Dot looked up. "You look pale. Aren't you and Amy friends?"

Carl stood transfixed. "It's not that Amy," he whispered.

"It's so nice to see you, Carl," Amy Dykstra said with a serene smile, sipping her coffee on the patio of Mo's, "You look good, really good."

"Thank you," Carl said, still trying to shake the surprise and discomfort he felt at Amy's sudden appearance, "I feel good. Listen, Amy, I want to say again how sorry..."

"Oh, Carl," she interrupted, "I know you're sorry. Don't worry. It was something you felt you had to do. You might have discussed it with me, but it doesn't matter. Here we are, having coffee in a lovely place. It's nice, isn't it? I can see why you were drawn to this place."

"Actually, Amy, I had no idea of this place. I just drove until I came to the ocean. This happened to be where I stopped when I got here."

"You didn't plan on coming here?" she frowned and sat back in her chair, "You didn't know ahead of time when you left?"

"No idea."

She regained her serene smile and leaned forward, "You must have been very frightened of the idea of marriage. I understand. It's a big step. I think I pushed you a bit too much, didn't I?"

"Well, no, not really," Carl responded, "We were engaged for a long time."

"But," she said, "moving from being engaged to actually getting married was scary, wasn't it?"

Carl was silent for a moment. He listened to the gull sound and the barking of the Sea Lions. *Relax,* he told himself, *You're getting pulled into a conversation she wants to have, not you.* He took a breath and spoke.

"Amy, I left Grand Rapids because of something pulling me, not because I was afraid of something. It seems from your perspective, I would guess, that I was running away. But from my perspective I was moving toward a way of life I wanted, but couldn't formulate, put into words. I had to move here to get the clarity I needed."

Once again, Amy frowned and leaned back, "I see. And have you found what you 'needed?'"

Carl once again was silent and listened to the waterfront. *Have you?* he asked himself, and immediately knew the answer.

"I have," he nodded.

"Oh," she said, "and just what is it you've found?"

She wants you to explain yourself. He was surprised at the clarity of his thoughts. *She wants you to justify your actions.* He smiled a little puzzled smile as he realized that he'd spent his life in weaving complex justifications, explanations, and excuses for not being what this or that person wanted him to be. He was very good at it and he was just about to do it one more time. Another deep breath,

"I really can't explain it. It's something inside that I know gives me joy and contentment."

He could see the motion of her mind reflected on her face as she processed, sorted, and revised her action plan. "Well, never mind. I'm just glad you're doing all right and I'm glad to see you. Does your boss mind your taking off work like that? I know I surprised you. I hope it's all right with her. She seems so nice and it's a beautiful little store."

"No," he said, "the work is flexible. We're getting ready for the summer rush. We get a ton of tourists beginning in a week or two."

"Oh, you're going to stay the summer?" she asked with another sweet smile.

"I live here, Amy," he said.

"Don't be rude," she frowned, "I was just asking you. I'm concerned for you."

Concerned for me? he wondered, *Does anyone really see me as I am?* Then he thought, *Yes. I am seen that way here by Coop and the others.*

He smiled with what he hoped was courtesy. "Don't be concerned. I'm happy and doing well, as I said."

The wheels continued to turn in her mind. "Well, good," she said with cheer and pep in her voice. "I'm staying at the *Whaler* - that's a nice hotel on the cliff looking over the ocean."

"I know the place," Carl said, "some friends own it."

"Oh, I'm so glad you have friends. That's good," she gushed.

Jesus! Carl thought.

"Uh, when do you have to leave," he asked.

"Oh," she chortled, "I've got a whole week free. You could take some time off and show me around. It's such a beautiful area."

About to choke, Carl looked up and saw Connie making her way through the tables toward them. Her wonderful smile replaced the ice in his chest with a warming thaw. "Connie!" he said loudly, "Hi."

Connie came up to their table and leaned over to kiss Carl quickly on the lips, something she had never done. "Hi, Carl," she said, looking into his eyes, "Dot said you might be here." She straightened and looked at Amy. "Is this your friend from Michigan?" she asked.

Oh, Connie, he thought with great affection and amusement, *I know you. You're up to something.*

"Yes. Amy, this is Connie. Connie, this is Amy Dykstra from Grand Rapids."

Connie extended her hand and Amy quickly grasped it and gushed, "Oh, I'm so glad to meet Carl's friends."

Connie held an amused expression and said, "Yes, Carl is deeply loved by people here. We're lucky he chose Carson Beach to be his home."

The wheels continued to turn. Carl was fascinated by the fact that he could see the process of shifting and strategizing appear on Amy's face. "Yes, well," she said, "I'm hoping he will take some time to show me around and let me in on what he's found so special here."

Oops! Carl thought, the smile is there but the words are slipping.

"He brought the specialness with him," Connie said calmly.

"Yes, well," Amy tried again, "I'm looking forward to seeing everything."

This has gone on far too long, Carl realized. He stood beside Connie and said, "Amy, you didn't let me know you were coming. You presumed that I would drop my life and do your bidding. I'm not going to show you around. I'm not going to entertain you. I'm not even going to be nice to you. I've apologized for hurting you a dozen times and tried to make it clear I'm done. Now that you're here, let me make it even clearer; I'm done!"

He turned to Connie, "Walk with me back to the bookstore." Connie smiled and took his arm.

"How dare you!" Amy shouted and stood up from the table. All eyes turned toward them. Connie squeezed Carl's arm and whispered, "It's fine, it's fine."

Amy picked up a water glass and tossed the contents toward Carl's face, but Connie had seconds earlier pulled him gently to the side and the water splashed across the floor.

Amy burst into tears and shouted, "You are not worth it. You are an awful man," she went on in a louder voice, "And you call yourself a Christian!"

In the stunned silence, Carl smiled and shook his head, "Actually, Amy,

I don't. Good bye." He put his arm around Connie and they walked out of Mo's to the sobs and wails echoing behind them.

Chapter 21 - The Horse You Rode In On

Cooper was slicing tomatoes for his famous tomato parmesan soup while Connie was taking a break in the kitchen for a moment before the lunch crowd began arriving. Soon the summer visitors would keep them both working full-speed along with extra help from Michael and Jeanette, the college students who worked part-time, more like full-time in the summers.

Carl opened the back door and stuck his head in the kitchen. "Mind a bit of company?" he said, "I'm willing to work for food."

"Come in," Cooper said, "you can fetch me a cup of coffee from the cafe, and pour one for yourself while you're at it. Then sit down and tell me about yesterday's encounter at Mo's. The grapevine is sprouting new leaves of gossip even as we speak."

"Oh, god," Carl groaned as he walked through the kitchen to the cafe.

"Oh, Carl," Connie patted his shoulder as he passed, "it's not so bad. A bit of water-tossing is mild for a Carson Beach spat. The gossips will have a full-fledged bar fight within another day or so to talk about."

"Great," Carl said from the cafe. He returned with two mugs of coffee and handed one to Cooper. "Some customers just came in Connie," he said.

"Thanks, I heard the bell," she said as she hurried out.

"Sit, Carl," Cooper motioned to a stool, "I'm out of the loop. Tell me the details. I hear you are a cruel heartless beast. Sounds fun. What's that like, anyway?"

"Ha, Ha, Coop," Carl grimaced, "It's not really fun. I didn't treat Amy kindly. I'm going to have to apologize to her before she leaves."

Connie stuck her head in, "Two bowls of chowder, Coop. And Carl, I heard what you said. Don't talk to her before you talk to me, hear?" She turned back to the cafe before Carl could respond.

Cooper finished chopping the tomatoes and slid them into a bowl. He looked at Carl, shrugged his shoulders and said, "Don't ask me. I just cook and clean and hesitate to ever interfere in the lives of others."

Carl raised his eyebrows.

"Well," Cooper continued, "hardly ever, and then only with the absolute best of intentions."

Carl smiled, "Connie doesn't hesitate, I've noticed."

Cooper ladled two large pottery bowls full of chowder and laid them on the counter to await Connie's return.

"Connie doesn't see it as interfering," he said, "she seems to see it as explaining to people what's really going on."

Carl laughed, "She used to scare me a bit with her intuition, or whatever it is. But now, somehow, I trust her. I don't know what it is, but I do. She has a lightness about her that makes her insights seem ordinary, if you can call them that."

Cooper began chopping green onions with a practiced hand, the knife moving so quickly that Carl wondered how he avoided accidents. "You ever cut yourself?" He asked.

"Not for quite a while," Cooper said, looking up, "But back at the retreat center in my first couple of years at the job of Head Cook, I was a bloody mess. Andy, the director, used to tell me there was no better mindfulness practice than to work with a sharp knife."

"I can imagine," shuddered Carl.

Connie came in and picked up the chowder bowls. "Carl," she said, "I'll be right back. We need to talk for just a sec."

"Sure, Connie," he replied.

"You know," Cooper told Carl, "Connie would say that the things she seems to 'know' are simply what we would 'know' if we could pay relaxed attention to what's going on."

"Have you ever had that sort of 'knowing,' that 'gut feeling?'" Carl asked.

"Occasionally," Cooper nodded, "We all do, I think. We just don't notice it, or we dismiss it. It's not really a gut feeling, the gut isn't the most trustworthy of organs. It's something different. Don't know how to explain it."

Connie returned and asked Cooper, "Coop, could you watch the front while Carl and I chat a bit? Won't take long."

"Sure," Cooper said and scooped the onions into a small bowl, wiped his hands, and went into the cafe.

"Let's go out on the patio," Connie took Carl's hand and led him out the kitchen back door and around to the patio overlooking the beach and surf. The morning fog had moved back out to sea and the sun was warm overhead.

Connie went directly to her point. "Carl," she said, "Amy called me this morning and we had a nice talk."

"You what!" Carl exclaimed, "oh, shit, Connie. I'm sorry."

"Not at all," Connie patted his hand, "It was a very helpful chat. You know, of course, that she doesn't love you, never has, really."

"She doesn't?"

"Of course, not. You knew that."

"I, uh, didn't know that. I mean, she cried her eyes out when I left and you saw her yesterday."

"Honey," Connie said, "those weren't the tears of a heartbroken lover. They were the tears of a frustrated woman who isn't getting what she wants, possibly for the first time in her life."

"You mean she wanted me, but didn't really love me?"

"She didn't want you, Carl. She wanted the man she assumed you could become, with her help, of course. You had, 'potential.' You knew all this. That's why you got in your truck and came here."

Carl was silent. Then he sighed, " What did she say to you?"

"That you were in a crisis and shouldn't be taken seriously; that you didn't know what you wanted; that if I was really your friend I would help you see what you really needed."

"God!" Carl moaned.

"Oh, she was very sweet as she outlined to me what I should do and what you should do. Oh yes," Connie continued with a smile, "she also said it would be unwise for me to be romantically involved with you because you were confused."

"God," Carl moaned again, "What did you say to her?"

"Oh, just that I was happily married to a wonderful woman, that you knew exactly what you were doing, that you were where you belonged, and that she could fuck herself and the horse she rode in on."

Carl stood wide-eyed. Connie patted his hand again and said, "I've got to get back to work. She's on her way back to Portland to catch an afternoon flight. And, by the way, I think it would be good for her if you never contacted her again. She needs to find an new project, and I would think she already has one in the works. You won't be on her mind much anymore." She turned and walked back into the kitchen.

Carl stood watching the dark blue of the ocean speckled with whitecaps. *Who,* he thought, *or what, is that woman going about masquerading as a sweet and gentle waitress?*

Chapter 22 - It's Time

"It's time to show these," Sam Hsu commented as he paused before the ink paintings Carl had strewn about his cottage. "You have four or five that should be displayed at Dorothy's store. For instance, this wolf face. It is a powerful expression of wildness. It has good economy of brush strokes and subtle shadings without excess effort."

Carl stood silent, a familiar vacancy in his stomach along with a sense of a similar emptiness in his chest. He wasn't ready for showing. He had only recently affirmed that he had, indeed, found a home. He didn't want to leave the safe feeling, the cozy unthreatened sense of comfort that his daily routine of painting, working in the bookstore, and sharing life with friends had brought to him. To venture out into a realm of judgment and evaluation from the external world was a terrifying thought.

Sam turned and looked at him, seeing the hesitancy in his eyes. "You are afraid, I think," he said. "People will not like your work, you think. You will be rejected, you think. What I say is right?"

Carl looked away, his throat constricting with a recognized, but unnamed, emotion. "I'm just not sure I'm ready," he said softly.

"And what sign will you receive that will tell you when you are ready?" Sam asked.

"I don't know," Carl shook his head, "I just don't think I'm ready yet."

"Perhaps you will feel ready when your teacher says you are ready?" Sam queried.

"Well…" Carl stammered.

"Well." said Sam, "It is settled then. I will gather the paintings I want and take them to Dorothy. She and I will decide together which will go on display and sale."

"Sale!" Carl exclaimed, "Sale? I can't sell them. I wouldn't know what to charge. No one would want to buy them. They're the work of a beginner..."

"Yes," Sam said, "they are the work of a beginner. That is the sign I have been waiting for. They come from your Beginner's Mind. That is why you are ready. You do not set the price. That is Dorothy's job. Let go of these now. They no longer belong to you. Begin to paint some more."

Carl leaned back against the table to prevent his legs, which had suddenly grown rubbery, from collapsing. Sam turned and began to browse through the paintings. "Go for a walk," he said with his back turned to Carl, "Come back in thirty minutes. I will be gone and you can go to work. Don't think, work!"

As he walked along the edge of the surf towards the steps that would lead up to the Beach Street and the Happy Frog, Carl felt a longing close to sickness in his chest and throat. He walked on by the wooden steps leading to the street, not wanting to walk into the atmosphere of the Frog until he could be sure that he would not break down in tears upon entering.

The morning was cool, but the sun had risen over the coastal mountains and his shoulders began to warm. *Sunshine on my shoulders makes me sappy,* he hummed to himself in his childhood version of John Denver's classic song. He always thought his words were better anyway. The chuckle that came, first to his mind, then to his throat, broke through the blockage and emerged into the morning air. He smiled, turned and walked back to the steps.

Cooper was preparing a vegetable soup base for the lunch menu while Connie and Mary were cleaning up the dishes from the breakfast rush. Two customers were lingering over coffee and watching the sunlight playing on the waves. Connie looked out the window and saw Carl walking up the steps.

"Carl has some news for us, I think," she said as she wiped a plate and stacked it in its place on the shelf. Carl waved through the window and

Mary opened the back door to invite him into the kitchen.

"Hello, Mary," Carl said, "Taking a day off?"

"Hi, Carl," Mary replied, "Not really, just helping out 'till lunchtime. Then it's down to the Sanctuary for what promises to be a long afternoon and night. Sacha is about to have her pups."

"Sacha?"

"Our she-wolf," Mary said, "I think you were drawing her that day a few months ago when you went with me to the Sanctuary."

"A she-wolf," Carl said smiling, "Yes, that makes sense. I didn't see anything but her eyes that day. I was hypnotized by them."

"Yes," Mary agreed, "Yes, you're right. She has the most penetrating eyes, wild eyes, eyes in which you can feel the primitive truth of all animals."

"You were drawing Sacha?" Connie asked, still wiping and stacking dishes.

"Yes," Carl said, "in fact, I used those brush sketches for a painting I finished a few weeks ago," He took a deep breath, "and apparently Sam thinks some of my work should be shown at the store. He's going to talk with Dot about it."

"Oh, wonderful," Mary enthused and threw her arms around Carl, hugging him. Connie turned from her dishes and smiled. Carl caught her eyes as he disentangled from Mary. She held his gaze and he felt a current of electricity flash up his spine. *What is it?* he thought.

Cooper walked around the counter and gave Carl a hug, lifting him a few inches off the floor. "Congratulations! If Sam says that you're ready, you are really ready. Can't wait to see your work."

"Well," Carl demurred, "I don't know if Dot will even want to show much of it. I don't know when… she's got lots of requests to show even one piece. I know. She is very selective…"

"Yes,yes," Mary patted his arm, "Come on, Carl, be excited."

Connie came over and took his hand, "Carl," she asked in a matter-of-fact voice, "What are you really feeling right now?"

"Nervous," Carl said.

"No," Connie said, "I mean, what do you really feel about your art right now?"

"Unsure," Carl said, unsure of his response.

"What do you really feel about your art?" Connie repeated.

Carl looked into her eyes again. *What is it?* he thought again.

"What do you feel?" she asked again, with a force in her voice that broke through his defenses.

He smiled broadly, "I like my work. I think it will go well in the bookstore and I think some people will value it. I'm delighted!"

"Yes," Connie said and returned to her dishes, "that's it."

Amy Hsu poked her head into the kitchen from the cafe. "Hey," she called out, "does anybody serve customers here or are we just in the way of your conversations?"

"We're celebrating," Cooper said, "Carl's going to have a show."

"I know," Amy said as she walked over to Carl, "Sam told me." She was dressed in civilian clothes, a summer dress that revealed her shoulders in a manner that made Carl forget for a moment what the subject matter had been.

Amy put her arms around Carl and kissed him. Carl kissed her back. Everyone in the kitchen was quiet as Amy and Carl entered a private world for a moment. *Yes,* Cooper thought, *He's ready.*

Connie stood on her balcony looking west to the picture postcard sunset. Mary stepped up behind her and slipped her arms around her waist, kissing the nape of her neck.

"You're thoughtful this evening," she murmured, "Is it the book?" Connie's secret pleasure was writing science fiction. She was reluctant to submit her stories for publication, but Mary considered her the heir to Ray Bradbury as the voice of literary science fiction. She was now working on a book which Mary hoped would find the light of day in the publishing world soon.

Connie laid her hands over Mary's and leaned back. "No, not really," she said, "The book is coming along fine. You know how I am, writing is like recess used to be at school. It's play time for me, no matter how the story is unfolding. No, I'm just thinking about…"

She turned in Mary's arms and faced her, putting her arms around Mary's neck. She looked at her spouse's eyes and asked, "Do you think I interfere too much?"

This is a trick question, Mary thought. She had been with Connie for too many years to fall into the tender trap of an innocent-sounding query. She was silent for a moment. "I'm not sure exactly what you mean," she responded, "but my honest answer is, no, I don't think you interfere at all, let alone too much."

Connie shrugged her shoulders, still locked in Mary's arms, "Of course I interfere. I'm always telling people what to do; always blurting our what I think."

"If we weren't saying what we think, we wouldn't be saying anything at all," Mary responded, "And between friends, tone and intention mean everything. Your tone is always loving and your intention is always authentic and compassionate."

Connie laid her head on Mary's shoulder. "I told Carl's ex-fiancee to fuck herself."

Mary chuckled, "I'm sure you said it with tenderness and compassion."

"I could have been less blunt, more kind."

"Are you sure that the bluntness of 'fuck yourself' wasn't actually the kindest way of getting your point across? Maybe you sensed she needed a figurative slap to get her attention."

Connie sighed, "Maybe. It's just that seeing, knowing, certain things isn't always easy. I know things, but don't always know what to do with that knowing." Soft sobs began to escape from her throat and she buried her face in Mary's shoulder.

"Sweetie," Mary murmured, "nothing's easy, but one of the many things I've learned from living with you for decades is that, if not easy, life is always interesting and wondrous. I love you so much."

Connie stayed snuggled against Mary for several moments of comforting silence. The soothing sound of the surf and the gradual approach of night creating a womb of security, shutting out the wider world for a time.

After a light dinner of cheese, fruit, marinated mushrooms, and Focaccia bread, they sat quietly on the patio as a full moon painted a narrow highway of light across the surface of the ocean. Connie sipped a glass of Pinot Grigio and Mary enjoyed a "wee dram" of Jameson's Irish Whiskey.

"Carl is so excited about his show tomorrow," Mary said, "I hope it is a giant success."

"It will be," Connie said, "Sam Hsu has spread the word to his friends."

"Oh," Mary said, "that sound's sort of frightening. Is Carl ready for a critical professional audience?"

"Sam wouldn't invite critics," Connie assured her, "Besides, he knows Carl's work is better than Carl thinks."

"Well," Mary said, "I'm still nervous. It's an important day for Carl."

Connie turned away and said softly, "Everything about Carson Beach is very important."

"It is? What do you mean?"

Connie's gaze focused on the distant horizon where the stars met the off-shore fog. "The world is going to shake loose of much of what people have come to take as permanent. A person doesn't have to have much prescience to know that. As that happens, it will be important for certain people to be together."

"You mean like us?" Mary reached out for Connie's hand.

Connie smiled, "Yes, like us. But more than that. Small communities of people are drifting together, not really knowing why, but unconsciously being drawn and preparing for very important work. It's happening here. I see it clearly and I need to do what I can to encourage it. That's why I've been… so interfering."

"That's why you think Carson Beach is important?"

"Carson Beach, The Happy Frog, everything around us… it's wonderful, but also very important. I don't know how… but it's Cooper, Dot, Carl, Ito, Kathleen, Kenny, Paul, Sam, Amy, and others I haven't seen yet but are going to be here, somehow.

"And Cooper is more important than he realizes. He has enjoyed making the Happy Frog into the wonderful haven it has become, but he underestimates his abilities. He's still feeling wounded after all these years. But pretty soon he's going to find that he isn't in Carson Beach just to be a happy cook at a Happy Frog."

"What else for him?" Mary asked.

"He is a brilliant man; something he hides even from himself. He will have to be more forthcoming in some sort of leadership. People want to look to him, but he stays reticent.

"That's natural," she went on, "but he'll need to open up a bit more."

"How?"

Connie laughed, "I really don't know. What? You think I know everything? I've told you for decades that we all know things we don't know we know. Damn, I wish people would wake up."

Her laughter turned quickly to tears, "I sometimes feel so lonely, so odd. I want to just relax, be your lover, love my friends, and enjoy my life and let someone else 'know things.'"

"Honey," Mary said, "You can't not know what you know. So just relax, be my lover, love your friends, and enjoy your life."

Connie sniffed and smiled again, her moods changing like the moonlight appearing and disappearing in the drifting clouds.

"I will. I do!" She turned to face Mary, "Everything is so exciting and wonderful. It's just that… I just want to… to get it right."

Mary cocked her head, "You really think it depends on your 'getting it right?'"

Chagrined, Connie lowered her eyes and giggled, "Of course it doesn't." She sighed and leaned back in her chair, "Of course it doesn't. I forgot that. How wonderful! Of course it doesn't."

She turned back to Mary. "Thank you for being you, love. Now finish your Jameson's and come to bed with me. We'll snuggle and let the world turn on its own, just for a while."

Mary stood and gulped the rest of her whiskey, "For a good long while," she grinned and took Connie's hand, pulling her up and into her arms.

Chapter 23 - Right Livelihood

Words and Images bookstore looked like it had been turned into Happy Frog II on the evening of Carl's show. Cooper had prepared a feast of the first order, with all of the tastes, aromas, colors and textures of the cafe somehow transported to the long table set across the back of the store.

Dot had closed the store at 5:00 PM to prepare and reopened at 7:00 PM to a crowd of people already lined up at the door. Carl was astonished at the crowd. He had expected a handful of friends and a pleasant intimate little start to his new life as an artist. He had forgotten or underestimated the connections and respect that Dot had gained during her years as patroness of the words and arts on the west coast. He also neglected to take into account the circles within circles represented by Kathleen and Kogan, Kenny and Paul, Connie and Mary, Cooper, Sam, Amy, Philip, and the other members of his new extended family.

His paintings had been expertly arranged by Sam and Dot in the front alcove and illuminated with just enough soft light to bring the viewer's attention to the blend of tones Carl had achieved with each brush stroke. He could not take his eyes off his own work, seeing it for the first time in a setting that communicated respect for its style and quality, a respect that was so difficult for a beginning artist to assign to his own work.

He felt a hand on his shoulder and turned to find Sam Hsu looking at him with an intent expression that was hard to read; Disappointed? Upset? Ready to deliver some bad news?

"Well," said Sam, "how are you feeling about all this attention?"

Is there a way I should be feeling? Carl thought, but answered truthfully, "Sam, I don't know. I really love seeing my work in this atmosphere. It makes me feel... well, like... I know this sounds silly, but like a real artist."

A smile opened on Sam's face, "Good," he said, then turned and walked over to where Amy, Cooper, Kathleen, and Ito were sitting.

"It's a matter of right livelihood," Ito was saying, "there is so much need for beneficial work in our world and so few so-called jobs that provide it. The preoccupation with 'getting a job' is a distraction from the reality of life on this planet."

"People have to earn a living, though," said Amy.

"Yes," Ito nodded, "though I tend to think that living is a given, a gift, not something earned. But I agree that basic needs need to be attained. What, though, are those needs, really?"

Cooper chimed in, "They're really very simple and actually not that hard to acquire - warmth, food, shelter, love, and meaningful work.

Dot had been standing nearby and laid her hand on Cooper's shoulder as she spoke, "We have a large group of people here in Carson Beach who are actually 'working' by Ito's definition, that is; doing good, creative, and helpful work without earning more than a basic living. Look at Cooper here. He has a law degree and he spends his days scrambling eggs and cutting mushrooms." She squeezed his shoulder and leaned over to kiss the top of his head.

"Important work," nodded Cooper, "There is so much work that needs to be done, and our culture offers us 'jobs' instead."

"Aren't jobs work?" Amy asked.

Cooper thought a moment, glanced over at Dot, took a deep breath and said, "Not very often. The concept of a 'job' is a product of the industrial revolution. Millions of people were persuaded by a combination of sophisticated propaganda and government pressure to leave their natural work, migrate to population centers, and take 'jobs.' It was a social revolution of great magnitude and it succeeded. That is, it made a few people very wealthy and the rest of the population into slaves. With rare exceptions, salaries, benefits, and working conditions are totally conditional. If the employer's bottom line is at risk, pfft! go the salaries, benefits, and then the jobs themselves.

"Even if the jobs are meaningful in and of themselves," he continued, "like yours, Amy. You do very important work that requires great skill, courage, and wisdom. But should the employer - in your case the State - face financial trouble, your fate is the same as anyone else's, no matter how important the job or how well you do it."

"There is that," Amy admitted, "but I do love the work I do."

"There you are," Cooper smiled, "You've turned what culture calls a 'job,' into true 'work.' That's the key, whether we call it a job or not, it must be true 'work,' or 'right livelihood' the Buddhists call it."

Carl spoke up, "I hope I'm in the category of right livelihood. This has been wonderful tonight. I realize that I don't need much to be happy. I'm warm, loved, and doing work I value and enjoy. I hope I can find a way to keep doing it and provide for myself all of my life."

Dot raised her eyebrows, "Well, Carl," she smiled, "you're on your way. We've sold three of your paintings so far, at $500 each. That's $500 for the store and $1000 for you. Should buy food for the starving artist for a few months."

Carl's mouth dropped open. "I didn't know we were charging that much! I... well, I..."

Sam chimed in, "Carl is right to be astonished. Such a low price was a mistake on our part. Dot, we must not let that happen again."

Carl looked to see if Sam was joking. His serious eyes without a glint of a smile showed that he was not. All Carl was able to do was shake his head and remain quiet.

Ito moved his hands excitedly in an open-armed gesture, "Exactly! That's just what I mean. Beyond those things our life should be about creating health, beauty, and community - not about earning more money and having more things." He paused a moment, then continued in a more somber tone, "Kat and I have been thinking a lot about right livelihood, about what good work really is. I love my work, but I don't love the medical establishment and I absolutely loathe insurance companies."

"Amen to that," Kathleen exclaimed.

Ito smiled at his spouse, "Anyway, we've been giving thought to some major changes."

"Changes?" Dot queried.

Kathleen nodded, "Yeah, pretty major. I have a bit over a year left before I can take early retirement. As much as I value my job, the constant rounds of child abuse, spouse abuse, even murder - all the dark side of our society is starting to wear on me. I'm actually getting tired of cleaning up messes. It's necessary work, but a person can only do it for so long. I'd like to see if some of the messes could be prevented. I'd like to be more proactive in helping people. Anyway, we're thinking of shifting our work in a year or two."

Cooper looked at them, "How would you do that?"

Ito responded, "We might find a place where I could establish my practice on a different premise. All I really need is a clinic big enough for an examining room, maybe two; a committed staff of nurse and receptionist; and enough money to pay my malpractice insurance, the rent, and a stipend to take home."

"What premise are you thinking of?" Cooper asked.

"Well," Ito responded, "Since our society is too screwed up to realize that it has a responsibility to provide health care to everyone - a "one payer" sort of health care, I think that I, at least, could behave as if such was actually the case."

"How?" Amy asked.

"By accepting patients who don't have insurance, or whose insurance is totally inadequate. By charging on a sliding scale and refusing to take insurance payments. By running a public clinic, so to speak.

Dot looked at Kathleen, "So what is your part in this shift that you and Ito are planning?

Kathleen took a deep breath, "Well, I'd like to dust off my Psychology degree and open a practice as a combination Social Worker and Private Detective. I think it's a combination that could bring some help to people and families that don't receive it or don't know how to look for it. We're thinking of renting a space in Carson Beach where we could house both his practice and mine. It will mean a dip in income but, why not? Sachiko is grown and moved out. We value a simple life. We just feel it is time to take a step toward the kind of world in which we'd like to live," she smiled and added, "You know, if I had an actual law degree I think I'd become a street lawyer.

"Street lawyer," Connie mused. She looked at Cooper and smiled, keeping her eyes on his, "That would be a very interesting way to use a law degree, wouldn't it."

"Jesus, Mary, and Joseph," Mary exclaimed in her best Irish brogue. She raised her glass in a salute, joined by everyone. "and all the saints preserve us," she toasted. "What's to become of us now?"

About the Author

William Martin is an award-winning author whose work expresses the practical wisdom and inspiration of Taoist thought for contemporary readers. He is the spouse of Nancy, the father of Lara and John, and the grandfather of Jillian and Andrew.

A native of California, Bill graduated from the University of California at Berkeley with a degree in Electronic Engineering. After four years working for the Navy as a research scientist, he returned to graduate school. He earned a Masters degree from Western Theological Seminary in Holland, Michigan. He did not find himself fitting within the Christian Church clergy structure so, guided by his love of the *Tao Te Ching*, he began to seek his own way. He spent two decades in private practice as a Marriage and Family Counselor in Phoenix, Arizona, and taught counseling for many years at Rio Salado College in Phoenix. He has been a student of the Tao for four decades.

In 1998 he and Nancy decided to simplify their lives so they sold most of their possessions, left their careers, gathered their remaining belongings into a 5X8 foot U-Hall trailer and moved to the Oregon coast. Nancy worked at a small Inn and Bill wrote a book. In 1999, after a year of strolling along the beaches, walking through the forests, and feeling the intense joy of the natural world, they moved to Northern California. They live a somewhat private existence, connecting with their close friends and with their individual work. They walk, read, enjoy qigong and cherish their life together. Nancy is a traditional bookbinder, restoring old books and creating hand-bound editions of new ones (www.nwbookbinding.com). Bill continues to write (www.taoistliving.com) and paint in the Taoist tradition.

Tales of the Happy Frog - The Beginnings is his first work of fiction.